KANGAROO COURT

KANGAROO COURT

MARK FURNESS

Liquorice Light Publishing

Mark Furness is a best-selling writer of thrillers, mysteries, and dark comedy crime.

He has worked as a journalist in the US, the UK, Australia, and East Asia. His stories often feature reporters, a prime example being the international conspiracy thriller, *Under Eden.*

Mark is Australian and based in Sydney.

Learn more at: www.markfurnesswriter.com

Kangaroo Court is Book 2 in the *Firefly Electrics Series* of dark comedy crime thrillers featuring electricians Lennie and Joe, and their cockatoo, Rawcus.

Firefly Electrics Series:
#1 Justice Machine
#2 Kangaroo Court
#3 Galaxy Motel

About Kangaroo Court:

Lennie, Joe, and Rawcus are touring inside a mountain forest when they discover an abandoned campervan – and a pair of stringless tennis racquets. Who would own such objects, and why? The deeper into the forest they venture, the more mysterious things they find. They're soon headlong on a mission to save strangers from a terrifying ordeal among the trees.

Meanwhile, their partner in a secret botanical business is abducted, forcing Lennie and Joe to confront demons from their past. Can they save the childlike young man they call The Chemist?

If that's not enough to juggle, their friend Pauline Gerrity rings an alarm from her refuge for abused women and children. Her call leads Lennie and Joe to create a sculpture they title *Cocoon of Man* and hang anonymously from an inner-city tree. A leading art critic likens their work to the British street artist, Banksy. But when the critic adds that the mysterious tree-hangers must be "borderline psychos", Lennie and Joe aren't sure whether to be flattered or insulted.

PART 1 - ETHER

1 - DRESS CODE

A WOMAN'S DRESS billowed as if a ghost was wearing it. The red and yellow costume waltzed above a dirt road inside a tall forest on a hazy afternoon. There was a human witness. Joe.

At the wheel of the rumbling Firefly Electrics van, he went drop-jawed.

Lennie dozed in the bucket seat beside him. Rawcus, perched on a wooden rod fixed between the headrests of the seats, missed the show too because a black sleeping beanie covered his feathered head.

Joe slammed his foot on the brake, throwing Lennie forward and clunking his freshly-shaven skull against the windscreen. Rawcus sensed the fast-changing momentum but couldn't stop swinging over to upside down. "Faark!" the cockatoo cried as his hood fell off.

"Sorry," said Joe, who opened his door and stepped barefoot towards a thorny, trackside shrub upon which the hibiscus-print frock had settled.

Aaaa!

At the childlike cry, Joe did a 360-degree turn, scanning patchy bush between the trunks of ancient gumtrees that squeezed both sides of the track. He could see neither man nor beast.

Lennie appeared beside him, rubbing a plum-coloured lump that was growing on his forehead. "Pig hunters?"

"Could be a pig," agreed Joe, who knew a cornered feral swine could howl like a child in pain, especially if it had a hunting dog's teeth clamped to its bum, which happened occasionally out here. "But I doubt it was wearing that," he said, nodding at the frock.

"We've seen stranger things," said Lennie, recalling a two-headed black snake he'd observed in the forest a few weeks ago. One head had been drinking from a puddle, the other head was keeping a lookout for trouble, though in hindsight Lennie conceded that a five-star hangover may have triggered double vision.

Joe peeled the short-sleeved dress off the shrub and held it up by the shoulders with banana-fingered hands that rendered the clothing doll-like in scale. The dress had a button-up front and was ripped down the back from the collar to the waist. "Someone was in a hurry to get this off."

"Passion?" Lennie suggested, entertaining optimism. He put his unusually rosy perspective down to the disorienting clunk of his head on the windscreen.

"Or the opposite," said Joe. "The wearer's not here to say."

"Jury's out then," said Lennie, who squatted and peered at tyre prints on the track. "Two vehicles," he concluded, fingering dirt then pointing. "Heading in that direction by the look of the spray. Fresh too."

Joe grinned. *By the look of the spray.* Lennie usually said this when he picked the wind direction while they sailed their little yacht, *Flamingo Sky,* on the open ocean. In a day or two, when their current mission was completed, Joe hoped once again to be whale watching from its deck at dawn. Right now, he sniffed a spanner falling into those works, but it was too early to tell how big, small, or stinky the spanner might be. The vehicle tracks turned left a couple of stone throws away, heading into a firebreak trail carved by an earthmover. The bush was making a comeback.

Joe started to retrace his steps to the van, intending to follow the tracks on wheels rather than by foot – not because he was shoeless but because they had precious cargo on board the Firefly that shouldn't be left alone, as well as Rawcus who would get inconsolably cranky if he was left behind when adventure lay ahead.

"What the hell?" barked Joe, sidestepping something dark and furry that was sliding along the gutter of the track.

If the hat-sized thing was alive, it didn't look like any creature that Joe had ever seen, even when he'd been on mind-altering adventures with Lennie, which was quite often. He thought that maybe last night's magic mushroom casserole with lamb shanks and sweet potato was staging a comeback. The blue-capped fungi had been packed with more surprises than a sack of firecrackers tossed into a campfire, which was one of Lennie's favourite party tricks and was on the menu for later tonight – if they could get to where they wanted to be.

Right now, however, Joe felt it wise to put a middleman between him and the 'thing' until its nature was known. He picked up a stick and poked it. It stopped. He lifted it into the air.

"Creepy," observed Lennie, who wasn't talking about the small, horny-backed lizard which scurried away after being revealed as the carrier of the miniature fur coat.

Joe examined his catch. "If it had blood on it, I'd swear there's been a scalping."

A red-back spider crawled from inside the wig of apparently human hair, making its way in an irritated manner along the stick towards Joe's hand. Joe watched the venomous creature step onto the back of his hand. The spider appeared to be juggling whether to run or fight. It bared its fangs.

"Help yourself," invited Joe. "But why waste your energy, buddy?"

Lennie shook his head, partly in admiration, partly in everlasting amazement, because Joe was immune to most types of spider bites. Doctors had done tests on him, but there was no chemical reason they could pin it down to. Joe reckoned he was bitten by different spiders so many times as a kid that the pain had been reduced to a feeling that was no worse than a mozzie bite. But Lennie knew that in Joe's mind, *spiders* could take many forms. Years ago, then schoolboy Joe, who was delirious during a bout of measles, told a GP that he had been bitten by a poisonous spider named Mr Darian, who was also Joe's headmaster. Boy, did the brown stuff hit the fan after that slant was put on matters?

Lennie got dragged into it by trying to cover up what Joe meant, fearing Mr Darian would twist the facts, which he did, of course. Mr Darian didn't get to be the master of 11-year-old kids like Lennie and Joe by being stupid, the boys learned. A couple of policemen talked to them, then delivered the boys to a team of smiling doctors at The Brain & Mind Institute.

The medicos' amazing brains didn't know what to make of Joe's wide definition of a spider and his claims that Mr Darian had bitten him, apart from asking sneaky questions and giving them inkblot tests. After that, the boys were filled with drugs that made them sleep for days on end.

Lennie and Joe could have done that deep-sleep shit at home in much greater comfort, they agreed later. So they hadn't spoken to any doctors since, not about brain health anyway. Doctors, they decided, were only good for fixing broken bones and stitching cuts. Lennie and Joe had decided to care for each other's brains instead, and so far it had worked out pretty well by their measure.

In the forest, Joe crouched and gently blew the spider from his hand into a pile of leaf litter. "This is shaping as a fair mystery," he said rising, holding the red and yellow dress in one hand and the black-haired wig in his other as if weighing possibilities.

"Cast-offs from a small, bald nudist?" offered Lennie.

Nie! Nie!

These screams caused Rawcus to wobble upon the rod in the van to which he had just returned using skilled but undignified wing work. Putting the sleeping beanie over his head unassisted was a trick he was yet to master. He dropped it, turning a blue-ringed black eye to the bush.

Nie!

"*That* was human," said Joe.

Lennie nodded.

The two men jumped into the van and Joe tossed the wig and dress into the back.

"Hang on," Joe warned as he sparked the ignition and floored the accelerator. Rawcus rolled backward like a gymnast on a crossbar with a casual approach to training. Joe well knew that Rawcus was mostly good-humoured if given fair notice that life was about to get bumpy, and bumpy it got.

"Hoo-roo!" cried Rawcus. "Woo-ha!"

The van leaped and fishtailed as Joe gunned off the main track and down the potholed fire trail. He spotted a parked campervan, painted with psychedelic stripes that reminded him of a rainbow Zebra he'd been reading about in a picture book for his adult literacy class homework. The back doors of the campervan were open, clothes and bedding and kitchen utensils were strewn upon the track.

Joe stopped behind the camper. "Looks like a bushwhacking," he said, combing his freckled fingers through his mop of red hair. They got stuck in the tangles. He cut the engine.

Lennie stroked the bruise on his temple as if it might be a sign of more sinister things to come. Hopefully not a tumour, he thought.

He and Joe slipped from either side of their mothership, landed on the soft earth, and looked and listened. Apart from a breeze rustling leaves, there was silence.

"Something's freaked out the locals," Joe whispered.

Lennie nodded. The absence of tweets, shrieks, and coos created a feeling at the nape of Lennie's neck like ants were crawling under his skin and nibbling his spinal cord. He massaged his vertebrae to squash the ants, taking no chances that they were real or imagined, and took a few steps forward, whereupon he squatted to examine the debris scattered behind the camper. The oddest things were two tennis racquets – with stringless heads.

Joe walked to the front of the camper. "Hey," he hissed backward at Lennie. "We have company."

"What company?"

"Police."

2 - THE BUSH WHISPERER

LENNIE WASN'T INCLINED to ask further questions. He was thinking about the home-grown marijuana they called Mars Grass that was sitting in a backpack in their van. He tip-toed backward, keeping whoever was in front of the psychedelic camper out of his line of sight so that he stayed out of theirs. He quietly opened the sliding side-door of the Firefly.

Rawcus eyed Lennie, who crossed a finger over his lips to urge the bird to maintain operational silence. Rawcus winked as if he got the message, although Lennie sometimes wondered if the bird simply had a nervous tic and in reality had no idea what Lennie was on about.

"Stay alert but not alarmed," Lennie whispered. Rawcus winked.

Lennie grabbed the backpack and pulled a throwing tomahawk from under the passenger's seat. Police officers could get pesky about drugs and weapons being carried in cars. Lennie pulled the sliding door quietly closed and backed into the undergrowth carrying his cargo, glad he was wearing jeans and heavy boots because snakes were plentiful on the forest floor in summer, and they liked to roam on hot, late afternoons like this. Some of the bastards even crawled in the overhead branches, occasionally hanging disguised like ribbons of bark. He heard a stranger's voice...

"We had a call-out to a burglary at a farm on Diamondback Road," the male said. "What's your excuse?"

"Sunday drive," replied Joe.

"It's Monday."

"Lost track of time."

"Anyone with you?"

"Not unless you count a cockatoo."

"Well, there's nothing here for you then. We have this in hand."

"We?" said Joe, raising his eyebrows.

"My partner's doing business in the bush."

Lennie's pulse kicked. He turned slowly, looking out for a squatting copper with his pants around his ankles, or a standing lawman clutching his dick. Nothing.

Lennie crab-walked, careful not to step on crisp sticks. He stopped behind a bush through which he saw the outline of the copper Joe was talking to. The forest behind him crackled and a thudding beat pressed in. He dropped the backpack and grasped the wooden handle of his tomahawk, swivelling to confront the attacker...

"What the fuck?" yelled the copper, who pulled his gun and aimed at the fast-approaching intruders.

A grey kangaroo as tall as a man bounced past Lennie and across the track near Joe and the copper, followed by two smaller bounders who, when they saw the humans, hit the panic button and crashed left and right into the scrub.

Lennie used the commotion to virtually step inside the thickly-leaved shrub beside him, a position from which he got a clearer view of the copper: he observed a fit-looking bloke in his mid-twenties, he guessed. The lawman was wearing a constable's light blue shirt and dark trousers, and was regulation-equipped: his utility belt carried a Taser, handcuffs, and a telescoping baton.

Joe said to the shaking copper, "New to the bush, are you mate?"

The sweaty-browed lawman reholstered his fat, black handgun and said to Joe, "How about you bugger off and have a good day?"

Joe turned toward the Firefly and began walking – on the spot. He was rubbish at the moonwalk, but he hoped his variation on the theme might do the trick. The copper headed in the opposite direction with quick steps. Joe ambled to the side of Lennie's shrub and pushed his shorts down. He looked at his manhood which had a helmet tattooed Hindu blue and spotted with yellow dots. Ah, the crazy things you do on your eighteenth birthday, thought Joe, who was glad he was now 33 and past his toadstool phase. Joe let it flow...

"Hoy!" hissed the bush. "I'm not waterproof."

"Sorry," said Joe, redirecting a stream fat enough to make a horse jealous. He spoke softly to the leaves: "There's a single paddy wagon up ahead. I saw it rocking."

"So you reckon they've got the owner of the wig and dress in there?"

Joe nodded. "I saw a red sandal on the track. Like my sister wore."

"You feeling heroic?" said the bush.

"Does the Phantom wear purple tights?" Joe replied, thinking about the cockroach-infested comics his dead dad left him, along with a damaged eardrum from childhood slaps that had been almost as regular as his heartbeat at times. The relevant ear itched, so he scratched it.

The bush whispered, "I'll stay here. You drive out to the main track. Then park and circle back through the bush on foot. And put some boots on!"

"Hey!" the copper called. He was standing back by the front of the Firefly. "What's with the bush whisperer act?"

"I have a brain condition," said Joe, who shook his hose and pulled up his shorts. "It makes me talk to trees with my dick in my hands. A type of Curette Syndrome, apparently."

"I think you mean Tourette," said the copper, who put his hands on his hips, drawing attention to the assorted artillery on his belt. "You've got two choices, smartarse. Hit the road, or I'll strip search you and your vehicle."

"I'll pick number one, thanks," said Joe, who was tempted by number two and smiled, wondering if the copper liked toadstools.

"Last warning, blockhead," growled the copper.

Joe put his hands up in mock surrender and climbed into the van, pulling his door shut. Before he could hit the ignition, a nerve-jangling cry echoed through his open window. Then a yelp, quickly muffled. The sounds came from the direction of the paddy wagon. Joe heard the crisp tap of metal-upon-metal and turned: the nose of the copper's gun was poking into his window and aimed at his head.

The copper said, "Step out of the vehicle. Don't be a hero."

Rawcus strutted along his rod towards the window. "Giss a kiss, love!" he blurted at the copper, poking his pointy pink tongue.

"What the fuck?" said the startled copper.

"He's just being friendly," said Joe. "You can always say, no."

The copper thrust his gun at Joe. "Get out!"

Rawcus squawked. "This won't end well, love! This won't end well, love!"

The copper shook his head at Rawcus. "Where does he get that crap from?"

Joe climbed out of the Firefly. "He grew up in a pub and he remembers stuff. He's got big ears."

The lawman snorted dismissively. "You feather-brains shoulda fucked off when you had the chance."

Rawcus had an ear cocked to the conversation. Joe sighed and stepped towards the front of the Firefly.

"Hey!" yelled the copper, who followed Joe. "Did I say you could move?"

Joe acted deaf, which was partly true. He took a few more steps and leaned back against the engine grill. The copper circled in front of him and aimed at Joe's chest with a double-handed grip.

Joe poked the tip of a little finger into his dodgy ear, pulled it out, and pretended to examine it for wax, all the while focussing his eyes beyond his fingertip onto the shrub inside which he hoped Lennie was still crouched.

"Turn around and face the van," the copper ordered, keeping his pistol in one hand while he reached with the other for the cuffs on his belt.

Joe noticed a glistening object spinning towards them from the forest.

The steel head of Lennie's tomahawk clipped the wrist of the copper's gun-toting hand. *Ka-thack!* The copper's wild shot echoed. The tomahawk crash-landed with a puff of dust and spun to a stop up the track. The copper squealed. Despite his torn flesh and chipped bone, the lawman held his pistol and used his good hand to lift his damaged appendage so he could renew his aim at Joe, who was sprinting at him.

Joe's snap-kick landed inside the copper's groin, connecting with more shinbone than foot, but it compressed his target's baby-makers with sufficient effect. Joe's follow-through lifted the man off the ground as he blasted another round that smashed through Lennie's bush.

The lawman doubled over, groaning. Joe grabbed him by his hacked wrist and squeezed; he figured he'd touched the nerve he was after when the copper yelped and dropped the gun, whereupon Joe head-locked him in the crook of an arm that covered much of the copper's jaw as well as neck.

Lennie emerged from the bush, checking himself for unwanted holes, and deciding there were none, he quickstepped towards the fallen pistol. He bent to pick it up.

An alien voice barked at Lennie from behind: "Don't fuckin' touch it!"

Lennie and Joe turned as one to face the speaker. Their eyes popped wide. A young white man, naked except for a pair of grey socks, was pointing his stiff penis to the sky and a pistol at them. He swung the barrel from side-to-side like he wasn't sure who to shoot first.

The gunslinger growled, "You ugly pricks have really stuffed up my day."

Lennie, sensing the nude nutter had been taking seriously good drugs, and possibly Viagra, given the proud state of his reproductive organ, said, "*That* is a very small cock you have."

The gunslinger's face took on a puzzled look and he stared down as if to see if this assertion had any foundation in fact.

"It looks like a red bantam," said Joe as dispassionately as a farmer judging livestock. "Not much to see when they're all plucked like that."

"Buck-buck, bu-gurk," chortled Lennie.

The gunslinger's eyes darted in various directions as if he was seeing and hearing things that weren't really there.

"Don't sweat, mate," called Lennie. "Best thing to do is hope you're hallucinating this entire scene."

The naked gunslinger started shaking.

Joe had a think: while Lennie's line of attack had clearly unbalanced the man, Joe was unsure whether this might cause him to take a pot shot at Lennie – or at Joe, despite his make-shift copper-shield – in an attempt to sift ghost from man, dream from reality. But then a vision began appearing before Joe, and he relaxed a little.

Behind the gunslinger, a naked young woman was step-ping as daintily as a ballerina. Her skin was as white as the inside of a new teacup, her shoulder-length hair a dark mess, and her eyes were black behind the tangled tresses that straddled her ghostly face. By her right leg, she was swinging Lennie's tomahawk, which in her hand appeared more like an axe. She was wearing a single red sandal. Joe tightened his arm-lock on the copper's throat, restricting his captive's vocal range to a gurgle and making his eyeballs almost pop from his head. The girl closed in.

Using both her hands, she took a backswing, and with an emphasis on accuracy over ferocity, she drove the hawk's blade into the gunslinger's skull.

"Shoulda. Fucked off!" cried Rawcus, who had climbed through the van's window and was eyeing proceedings from atop the Firefly's wing mirror.

3 - THE END OF THE WORLD

LENNIE took a butter-yellow blanket from the back of the Firefly and draped it over the shuddering girl's shoulders. Knotting her fists into the blanket's corners, she clutched it across her chest and wore it like a cape.

In a scratchy voice, for there were purple-blue bruises on her throat, she said, "Karl," and began retracing her steps along the track.

Lennie followed, carrying the pistol that Joe's copper had dropped. He flicked the safety catch off and rested a finger on the trigger, eyes wide open.

*

Back on the battleground, Joe kept a headlock on his copper and reached with his spare hand to the lawman's front, enabling him to unclip the laden utility belt which thudded into the dirt. Joe dragged his captive to the side of the dead body where he leaned down and took the pistol from the corpse's grasp.

Joe released the living copper, who dropped to his knees and put a hand on his colleague's shoulder before softly saying, "Jacko?" as if the enquiry might cause the corpse to miraculously spring back to life.

"You believe in zombies, do you?" said Joe. "I think it's Hollywood bullshit myself, but each to his own."

"What?" said the copper.

"Sorry," said Joe to both the dead and living. He put his insensitive wisecrack about zombies down to shock.

But just the same, this was no time to be sooking it up and over-thinking. Joe focused on the task near his feet. "I'm going to need this…"

Holding the gun in one hand, Joe leaned over and used his spare paw to grasp the tomahawk by its wooden handle. He tried to extract its stainless-steel head from the back of the man's skull in a respectful manner; this led Joe's little finger to point out straight as if he was drinking from a delicate china teacup in the Queen-of-England style that Lennie's Aunty Doreen had trained him to do on special occasions, such as wakes after funerals. The hawk stayed stuck.

"You might want to turn away for a moment. Or not. Up to you," said Joe as he placed a bare foot gently, then increasingly firmly, on the man's neck to stop his head lifting off the ground as he tugged the hawk. The copper swooned. Joe jiggled the blade free.

"I'll let you have a private moment now," Joe said solemnly, doing his best to impersonate a sensitive funeral home attendant.

Joe back-stepped, keeping an eye on both corpse and mourner, and sat on a fallen tree trunk. He slammed the bloodied hawk's blade into the timber beside him and rested the pistol on his other side. He figured the grief-stricken copper wasn't going anywhere soon. And if he did decide to scarper, Joe had the tools handy to make it a short run.

Rawcus flapped from the Firefly's wing mirror and landed on the log next to Joe.

"What a day," said Joe, shaking his head.

"What a day!" said Rawcus.

Joe stroked his companion's sulphur crest. It was now pretty clear to Joe who the ripped dress belonged too, but she had a good head of hair. The identity of the owner of the wig remained a mystery that made him fidgety.

*

Lennie glanced back at Joe and Rawcus sitting on the log, and the kneeling copper who was holding his fingers to his colleague's neck as if he might yet find a pulse. Lennie sighed: this track, which eventually led to his and Joe's hideaway at the place they had dubbed *No1, The End of the World,* had a knack of turning simple days into weird ones, which was part of its attraction. But how high could the weirdness dial go today?

Lennie twirled, scanning the scene in which he found himself: it reminded him of a glossy book about Australian artists he'd picked up last weekend at a junk market in the city. The pages were chock full of paintings by men and women who called themselves Surrealists. There were some by a bloke who made paintings about the long-dead bushranger Ned Kelly, most of which consisted of a black stick figure wearing a box helmet with a slot in the middle to let Ned see out. Historians reckoned Ned's real helmet had been made of iron to protect his electricity-driven, command-centre from being minced by hunks of flying lead as he shot it out with a mob of coppers over a hundred years ago. Ned wore an iron breastplate too, Lennie recalled. And iron underpants? Mm. Lennie couldn't remember that item, but given that men's brains were in their balls, as his late Aunty Doreen had often reminded him, a pair of iron undies would have been smart.

Lennie dug into his own skull: what was that painter's name? He was pretty sure it rhymed with steak and kidney... Sidney! Yes, Sidney Nolan could have done justice to this scene – too bad he was residing in the same dimension as the copper who'd been wearing the tomahawk hat.

Lennie looked around. There were top-notch ingredients for a Surrealist to work with: the long rays of a pink sun falling behind the trees against patches of a powder-blue sky; spidery shadows; a dead man with a stubbornly stiff penis wearing only his socks, his axe-riven head resting in a maroon pool; and a barefoot, red-haired giant named Joe, wearing a red-green, tie-dyed T-shirt and orange board shorts, sitting on a log beside a sulphur-crested cockatoo. Add to that a kneeling copper dressed in a light-blue shirt and navy-blue trousers, hunched over the dead man.

And behind that stage, there was a rainbow-striped, ransacked campervan, and a naked girl, caped in a yellow blanket, black-eyed and tangle-haired... Focus on her, Lennie told himself. *Help the girl!*

Lennie approached the blue-and-white-checked police paddy wagon: the back door to the mobile prison cell was wide open; there was a pile of clothes and a pair of black boots on the floor.

The girl squatted at the side of the wagon beside a shoeless, human figure which was seated in the dirt and leaning against a back wheel.

As Lennie closed in, he concluded the figure, dressed in blue jeans and a black T-shirt, was most likely a man. One of his wrists was handcuffed and chained to an eye-bolt attached to the side of the wagon. His head resembled a pale eggplant spattered with scarlet paint.

4 - BLUBBER BOY

THE GIRL stroked the man's bald skull and whispered to him in a language Lennie didn't understand, although he did make out the word "Karl" in the mix. Karl's face had a couple of purple slits where the eyes should have been. A blood-stained white tooth sat on the dirt beside him.

Generous bastards, these coppers, thought Lennie: they had cuffed just one of Karl's hands to the side of the paddy wagon, leaving him with a loose fist and the sense of a fighting chance as they monstered his girlfriend, just out of his reach but well within earshot, and within eyesight too if he stood and looked through the paddy wagon's cell window.

Lennie searched the wagon's front cabin for handcuff keys but couldn't find any in the usual places. He opened a small drink cooler that was sitting between the seats: it contained four cans of Cutter's Lager on ice. Flash buggers, he thought. Cutter's Lager was craft beer. Tasty on a hot day. Two empty cans lay crushed on the floor. Stuffed under a seat he found a drawstring cotton bag about the size of a sock.

"Well, hello little feller!" he said as he shook the contents onto a seat. He picked up a small, brown-stained glass smoking pipe and sniffed it. It had the whiff of paint thinner. Crystal meth, he guessed. Maybe heroin. He had a quick think; judging by the two coppers' bug-eyes and their agitated minds, he opted for the meth. He wondered how Sid Nolan might have incorporated these new elements into a painting if he had an easel parked trackside.

He carried the drink cooler to the side of the wagon and placed it next to Karl and the girl. "I'm going to keep looking for the cuff keys," he said.

"Mia," she replied, pointing at her chest.

After telling her his name, Lennie left her to soothe Karl's face with ice cubes from the cooler, using the cotton pipe-bag as a sponge that she dipped in the cold water.

Lennie returned to the clearing where Joe sat on the log guarding the living copper who was sobbing tears over his dead mate. Rawcus was patrolling above them on the branch of a ribbon-gum tree.

Joe puffed on a reefer of Mars Grass and nodded at the bawler. "Reckon he's acting?"

Lennie raised his eyebrows as if his answer to Joe's question was fifty-fifty. He took the joint Joe offered, toked, jawed out a few smoke rings, and called to the copper, "You and your mate have transported us all to a very strange place."

The copper sobbed. "It was a mistake."

"What?" said Lennie, coughing with feigned shock. "You mean you accidentally bushwhacked these kids, and raped the girl?"

"It was Jacko's idea."

"Oh, that's handy," said Lennie. "Blame a dead man who can't defend himself."

"It's true."

"Where are the cuff keys?" Lennie barked.

The copper stood but kept his face down. "The cuffs on that guy are Jacko's. But I've got a spare key."

The copper reached into a trouser pocket and tossed the key to Lennie. Lennie handed the joint back to Joe and set off for the paddy wagon.

Joe studied blubber boy, who kept staring down at his uninteresting black boots. Why was this guy doing everything possible to avoid eye contact?

Joe lifted the utility belt off the dirt and laid it across the log beside him. He extracted the Taser from its holster. It was as light as a water pistol. On its handgrip, it said *ZZ Novelty Co.*

5 - CRYSTAL BALL

LENNIE un-cuffed Karl, and helped him to stand and lean against the paddy wagon.

"Da," said Karl, massaging the wrist that had been chaffed from his struggles against the restraint.

Lennie climbed into the wagon's cell and sifted through the dead policeman's clothes. In the right front trouser pocket, a pair of woman's underpants had been stuffed. This copper was a souvenir collector, Lennie figured. But he carried no wallet, nor ID that Lennie could find. He climbed out.

He draped Karl's good arm over his shoulder and helped him walk towards the rainbow camper. The blanket-covered girl shuffled zombie-eyed beside them. At the back of the van, a folding chair had been dumped on the ground. Lennie sat Karl in it. The girl climbed into the van and said to Lennie, "Dressing." He pushed the double back doors closed.

"You alright if I leave you to it?" he said to Karl, who wobbled his eggplant head in the affirmative.

Lennie had another dig around the front cabin of the paddy wagon. Under the passenger side floor mat, a piece of rubber carpet was loose along the door seam. Lennie peeled the carpet back: recessed into the metal floor, there was a screwcap the size of a jam jar lid. He unscrewed the cap and put his hand into a small chamber from which he extracted a leather wallet. He had a quick look inside and tucked it into a pocket of his jeans.

When Lennie got back to Joe's clearing, swarms of flies were feasting on Jacko's cranium. While Lennie reckoned the gutless rapist deserved the attention of his newfound friends, the sights and sounds made Lennie's skin itch and crawl. He went to the Firefly and collected a canvas drop sheet, plus a bandage from the first-aid kit.

"Here," said Lennie, tossing the sheet and bandage to the copper. "Cover your mate up before the bushies eat him. But don't read too much into the bandage. *You* are facing a very uncertain future."

Joe didn't like blubber boy's body language, the way his eyes darted about the bush as he bound his wrist. Joe picked up a stick and tapped it on Lennie's boot. After securing Lennie's attention, Joe scratched a string of letters into the dirt near his feet.

Lennie grinned. No wonder Joe had just earned a gold star in his adult literacy class at night school. He'd just written "runner?" in the dirt.

The copper finished his first-aid and eyed the forest, his body twitching.

"Try it," called Joe, tapping the handle of the hawk that remained jammed beak-first in the log.

Lennie said to the copper, "How come your mate isn't carrying any ID?"

"What do you mean?"

"I just looked through his clothes. No wallet. Nothing."

"Those tourists must have stolen it. Gypsy fucking thieves."

"So what is Jacko's full name?"

"Ah..."

"What?" said Lennie. "You forgotten him already?"

"I'm in shock, mate. For God's sake. It's John Wilson. Jacko for short."

"And yours?"

"Constable George Ablett."

"Well, Georgie Porgie. That is a very interesting name. Had it long?"

"Twenty-six years."

"Mm," said Lennie, rubbing his chin. "There are a lot of ways we can handle this situation...how many do you reckon, Joe?"

"More than I can get a handle on at the moment," said Joe, who was usually excellent at numbers. Joe stood: "I've caught a terrible thirst. I need to deal with it."

"That disease is catching," said Lennie. "What about you Georgie? Want a beer? Think of it as a wake."

George nodded. Joe walked to the Firefly and climbed into the back cabin. He plucked three icy cold cans from a cooler, and turned to step from the van: Rawcus was standing on the dirt staring up at him.

"You don't miss a trick, do you?" said Joe.

Rawcus shot a schoolteacher look at Joe. Joe reversed and took a recycled tuna tin from a cabinet drawer. The tin had ® etched into the metal.

Joe climbed out of the van and held his hand down. Rawcus jumped on and tottered to Joe's shoulder. Joe carried the beers and the shallow tin.

"Giss a kiss, love!" said Rawcus, nuzzling Joe's ear.

Joe's eyes went a little dewy at the memory of Aunty D who taught Rawcus to speak as a baby bird. She and her friends at the Rose & Thistle had gifted the little feller with quite a vocab by the time she died 23 years later and handed guardianship of Rawcus to Lennie and Joe.

Back in the clearing, Joe opened a beer and splashed a thimble-sized dash into the tin which he placed on the dirt. Rawcus wet his beak and chortled, "Cheers, mate! Cheers, mate!"

Lennie plonked his bum on Joe's log and tapped the spot beside him. "Sit," he ordered Constable George Ablett. George shuffled over and sat.

Joe stood in front of them and handed over the beers.

Lennie turned to the constable. "We have a serious problem."

"Murder is pretty serious," agreed George, popping the seal on his can with a shaking hand. "And you attacked a police officer with an axe," he added, waving his bandaged wrist.

"Wrong problem." Lennie reached into his jeans back pocket and pulled out the wallet he had discovered under the paddy wagon floor.

"You look more like this bloke than a George Ablett," said Lennie, opening the slim pouch and extracting a photo driver's licence from which he read the name: *Robert Peter Hogg*.

"And your mate looks more like *Arthur Sylas Beck* – than Jacko Wilson." Lennie plucked another card and flashed Beck's photo licence.

"All right," said the copper, who wiped his frothy mouth with the back of a hand. "We're working undercover. These people with the campervan are drug dealers."

"Now we are getting somewhere, Robbie," said Lennie. "So where does sexual assault come into your work?"

"You've read everything all wrong," said Robbie, who burped. "Arty was the one who was assaulted. Neither of you guys actually saw him raping the girl, did you? They have a gun, you know. And they are actors. Look..."

Robbie unbuttoned the top pocket of his shirt and extracted a glossy pamphlet which he unfolded. He handed it to Lennie.

Lennie read the advertising spiel aloud: *See Poland's leading mime and contortionist act at the Redcliffe Valley Community Club this Friday night. Watch Mia and Karl climb through the head of a tennis racket...*

Joe rubbed his chin. "That might explain the stringless tennis rackets behind their camper."

Lennie tucked the pamphlet into his back pocket and drained his beer. "Tell me, Robbie. What sort of cops go undercover – dressed as cops?"

Robbie looked into his can as if it might be a crystal ball into his future. "We are working for internal affairs...there are bent officers out here smuggling methamphetamine into the city through a network of backpackers who bring it from interstate and overseas."

Lennie nodded. "So you need to smoke the stuff yourselves to make sure you've got the real McCoy?"

"Ah," said Robbie. "So you found the evidence bag with the pipe in it?"

"Tell you what, Robbie. You finish your drink and conjure up some decent facts, while I go and check on your victims, or the villains, as the case may be. My friends will keep you company. And when I come back, we'll chat again."

Rawcus danced around his near-empty tin of beer. "This won't end well!" he screeched at no-one in particular, before plunging his beak back into the amber fluid.

As Lennie stepped away towards the camper van, Robbie smiled at Rawcus and said to Joe, "How cute."

Joe looked at Rawcus like a proud parent watching their kid in a school play... Robbie pushed from the log like it was a starting-block for an Olympic sprint – and raced towards the kangaroo trail into the forest of ribbon-gums.

6 - THE VET

JOE COUGHED BEER and spat out the words "cheeky bugger". He glanced at the tomahawk and the pistol atop the log. They seemed to be saying, "Choose me! Choose me!"

Joe selected a tennis-ball-sized rock from among a few near his feet. Robbie skidded in mud on the track which slowed him, but he didn't fall; he bolted towards the roo trail, rushing under branches from which peeled bark hung like streamers and stroked Robbie's head.

"Tree snakes!" roared Joe.

Joe's cry caused Robbie to duck and look up, apparently fearful that one of the bark straps might in fact be a serpent. Joe stood and unleashed: the flying rock thudded into the skull behind Robbie's ear – his body dropped like he'd been shot.

"Whacko!" cried Rawcus, observing the hit. He moved to get a closer look – and stepped on the rim of his empty beer tin, flipping it into his face. "Watch out!"

Joe rolled his eyes at the bird and ambled across the track to where Robbie lay, moaning. In the mayhem, Robbie's shirt had untucked from his trousers, exposing a manufacture's label that Joe honed in on. He found it more interesting than the name of the Taser-maker, *ZZ Novelty Co*. He grabbed Robbie by an ankle and dragged him back to camp.

Joe was pleased with his choice of weapon – he had selected a lump of soft-ish sandstone instead of iron-hard granite. Joe regarded his work like that of a vet with a tranquiliser gun as opposed to a hunter wanting a head for his trophy wall.

7 - KANGAROO COURT

LENNIE, arriving back at the psychedelic camper, found Mia dressed in a fresh hibiscus-print frock in shades of purple and sky-blue. She and Karl were sitting on the floor inside the open back doors of the van with their feet dangling over the orange dirt. The two slits in Karl's face had opened enough to reveal that he was grey-eyed. He and Mia were sharing the contents of a brown glass bottle that looked to Lennie like a long-neck of beer, but it had no labels and was capped with a ceramic stopper that clip-locked with wire.

"Feeling better?" Lennie said, noticing that Mia's pupils were as big as coat buttons.

"Ya," she replied, offering him the bottle.

Lennie took a swig. "Whoa!"

He sniffed the top of the bottle. "Ether?"

"We call *light of blue*."

Lennie had swilled a bit of homemade ether in jail. It had taken him on quite a trip. It wasn't as perky as the LSD that a social worker had couriered into the prison from time to time under the collar of a long-haired, companion-Labrador. Still, the ether he had sampled courtesy of the State had a decent kick and he'd become partial to it during his stint for defacing a Catholic church and tossing a condom filled with red house paint that burst upon the Archbishop of Sydney with whose friends Lennie had become forcibly and intimately acquainted as a child.

He had another swig, grabbed an extra, and returned the bottle to Mia. Taking the advertising pamphlet from his jeans pocket, he waved it at Mia. "This you?"

"Ya," she said. "Karl and I are from Gdansk."

"How did you get here?"

"Uncle and aunty in Sydney."

"I mean here," he said, opening the palms of his hands to the surrounding bush.

"We lost our ways on picnic. Police appear. They say, *follow us to be safe in town*. They bring us here."

"The police say that you are drug dealers and thieves."

"What you think?" said Mia, offering Lennie the bottle of blue light.

He took it and swigged. "Do you have a gun?"

"I wish." Mia smiled thinly, accepting the boomeranging bottle.

Lennie admired an orange, red, and yellow halo that started to radiate from the perimeter of her body, as if a rainbow was hugging her. Lennie figured there was an ingredient in Mia's ether that was bigger than blue light and quite pleasant on the optic nerve. Karl's face now looked more like an orangutan's than a bruised vegetable. Lennie liked rainbows and orangutans.

As time lost meaning, Lennie's admiration for the ether and its owners started to blossom in a variety of ways, not the least of them being the way the forest was resembling a Vincent Van Gough painting, rendered with the Dutchman's trademark bold brushstrokes in vivid colours. Leaves and grasses danced slowly, as if underwater. Mia offered him the bottle and he took it, trying not to appear eager.

"Popular drink in Poland," Mia explained. "My uncle has a 'stillery in Sydney. In his garage. He is scientist at university."

"A handy skill," replied Lennie. "I have a friend who is a chemist. He does interesting work from home too. Do you have more of this fine vintage?"

"Does Pope wear white dresses?" Mia replied. She climbed into the back of her van and returned with an unopened brown bottle.

Lennie squinted. "Why put blue light in brown glass?"

Mia smiled. "Sunglasses, Lennie. Stopping burning from eye in sky."

Lennie nodded.

Mia sighed. "What we do with dead man? I go to jail?"

"We question the policeman first," said Lennie. "Can you and Karl help?"

"Oh, look!" she called, pointing into the bush.

Lennie's heart galloped and he spun around, looking for a multi-coloured SWAT team charging from the scrub to rescue their besieged mates by firing a meteor shower of bullets. Instead, a brown-eyed kangaroo peered at them over the top of a shrub. The animal winked, or so it appeared to Lennie.

"Excellent idea," said Lennie. "We shall have a Kangaroo Court."

8 - BLANK CANVAS

THE AIR COOLED quickly in the long shadows of late afternoon.

Lennie invited the lean Poles to join him and Joe in the clearing, after they had added warmer clothes to their frames. Mia insisted that Lennie take the fresh bottle of blue light. This pleased Lennie, who assured himself that the elixir would not affect the impartiality of the Kangaroo Court. In fact, he believed it would enhance it.

As he approached the clearing where the dead man lay under the tarp, Lennie was puzzled by the sight of Joe and Robbie, who was sitting wobbling on the log.

Joe, standing in front of the policeman, had stuffed the pistol by the barrel into the back waist of his board shorts whereupon the weapon jiggled in the makeshift holster of Joe's ample bum-crack as Joe busied himself wrapping a bandage around Robbie's head, working across the lower rear of the skull and anchoring it to the highpoint of the forehead, giving Robbie the appearance of a poorly wrapped Egyptian mummy – or the head of one at least. Robbie's good hand grasped the handle of the tomahawk and jerked its head from the log…

"Haawk!" Lennie yelled, accelerating into the clearing.

Joe, appearing deaf to the cry, tucked the end of the bandage into its own bindings to secure it on Robbie's skull. Robbie took a backswing…

Joe casually grabbed the copper's wrist. Robbie squealed and the hawk fell, forcing Joe to dance the quickstep to prevent the blade from slicing his bare toes.

"Are you crazy?" said Lennie, arriving bug-eyed. He bent to pick up the hawk.

"Hey!" barked Joe. "Don't touch it, mate. The murder weapon is covered in this bloke's fingerprints now."

"You cunning bastard." Lennie grinned.

"Cunning bastard," echoed Rawcus, stumbling along the branch above the sitting log.

Robbie moaned and slid forward off the log, landing bum down, leaning back against the fallen trunk with his legs spread.

"Don't you dare," said Lennie, eyeing Robbie who was eyeing the hawk in a covetous way.

Joe stepped to the Firefly and returned with an empty plastic shopping bag. He put a hand inside the sack and used it as a glove to pick up the hawk, folding the sack over the entire handle and head. "Evidence bag," explained Joe.

"You're quick to pre-judgement," said Lennie.

"What do you reckon?"

Lennie raised an eyebrow. "And what about the girl's fingerprints?"

"Up here for thinking," said Joe, tapping an index finger on his temple. "Already cleaned 'em off with a metho-soaked rag to give Robbie a clean strike on a blank canvas."

9 - LORD OF THE RINGS

LENNIE SWIGGED ETHER and looked up at Rawcus on the branch. His white-feathered body sparkled like a night star and the Mohawk plumes atop his skull glowed neon yellow with a delicious hint of violet.

Lennie wondered if he should splash a dash in Rawcus's tin to give the bird a keener perspective too, but he thought better of it. Rawcus got wild enough on a few drops of beer.

Joe looked at the bottle his childhood friend was cradling.

"Homebrew," Lennie explained. "Polish recipe."

"Any good?"

"Enlightening," said Lennie, handing the bottle to Joe.

Joe sniffed. "Smells like petrol." He took a gulp and passed it back to Lennie. "Tastes like it too. Could use some coke and ice."

"We're not bogans," Lennie said, rolling his eyes at the suggestion of adding such pollutants. He looked up at Rawcus. "Jesus, he's turned pink."

Joe saw the rosy hue too. Surely Lennie's brew wasn't that fast-working. He studied their surroundings. "I think it's the sunset, mate. Reflecting off the little feller." Joe pointed at a blood orange sky behind the tall trunks and sparse leaves of the ribbon-gums.

"Ah," Lennie sighed with an orgasmic smile. "The old sky painter has added sunsets to his repertoire." He was thinking about Delling, the Norse God of Dawn who fathered a son named Day with the Goddess of Night, and of whom he was a great admirer.

"Reper-what?" said Joe, who'd not come across this word before, not even in his night school classes.

Lennie, who'd been taught alongside Rawcus to collect words of all shapes and sizes by his Aunty D, said, "It means your skillset. You know...you're good at growing geraniums – now you've added petunias to your *repertoire*."

Joe decided it was a wanker's word. And while he liked the idea of the Norse sky-painter and his family, he thought that if the old guy existed – and he was yet to show himself in person to Joe, an act which Joe regarded as crucial if he was to be persuaded to believe in him – Delling should stick to mornings and give someone else a go on the sky at night. "Don't stray too far into space," he said to Lennie, who took another swig. "We have unfinished business here on earth."

Mia, carrying another long-necked brown bottle, led Karl into the clearing. She was wearing a woolly jumper but still hugged herself against the arriving cold.

Lennie shook his head and slapped his cheek as if he was breaking a spell. "Let's light a fire and get this court underway."

Robbie, his bum still in the dirt, tilted his unravelling mummy-head at Lennie. "What court?"

"We are going to have a trial," said Lennie. "And you're on the stand."

"This is madness," said Robbie, who hugged his knees against his chest as if the ball shape might protect him.

"Too right it is," said Lennie. "You and your mate, Arty, flicked that switch."

Mia said, "I will get wood for fire." She stood her bottle in the dirt, helped Karl to sit on the log, and stepped towards the forest fringe.

Lennie said to Joe. "Bailiff, will you please take appropriate steps to secure the accused?"

"Righto," said Joe, winking at Robbie before heading towards the Firefly.

"Oh," Lennie called after him, "can you bring some fire starter too?"

Robbie blurted, "She's the murderer," and pointed at Mia who was bundling sticks.

"Save it for the judge," said Lennie, who now regretted not bringing on this trip the shoulder-length wig made of blonde rope that he had knotted at the kitchen table at home for a previous trial involving an accountant. On that occasion, the trial – which was conducted at sea aboard the *Flamingo Sky* – had been carefully planned over months. Tonight's event was impromptu so he would have to improvise.

A courtroom operated by the State – and Lennie was familiar with them of course because, as well as studying them on TV, he had been in the dock of a real one – was full of theatrical props like wigs, and black gowns and gavels aimed at letting the participants know who-was-who in the pecking order. Without order, pecking or otherwise, there is chaos, he reminded himself, and as interesting as chaos is from time-to-time, now was not the time for it. So Lennie needed props. But what?

Joe – in his role as the court's security officer, and wondering what weirdness lurked around the corner in that place called *the future* which his adult literacy class teacher had recently discussed in a way that left Joe no wiser – entered the back of the van and grabbed a folding camp chair. Then he collected an empty plastic milk crate into which he put a roll of gaffer tape and a small can of petrol.

Back in the clearing, Joe unfolded the chair, which had armrests, and placed it opposite the sitting-log, nominating an empty spot near the log and the chair for Mia to arrange a pyramid of twigs and branches.

"Nice shape," said Lennie, who approved of the way Joe had arranged the log, chair, and fireplace. Lennie picked up a long stick and scratched lines into the dirt to link the objects and form a square, the log creating one side, the chair and fire marking the opposing corners. "The court is now in session!"

Joe nodded at Robbie, then nodded at the chair: "Get in."

Robbie grunted, "I'm happy here."

Joe huffed with disappointment. "You've got until Friday...Monday, Tuesday, Wednesday, Thur..."

Robbie hopped up and flopped into the chair. Joe started gaffer-taping Robbie's forearms and wrists to the armrests.

Lennie had a brainwave that he decided not to reject: he stepped to the Firefly and collected a black plastic bucket that he emptied of ripped packaging from screws and electrical plugs and other things which he and Joe used to run their electrician's business. Taking a box cutter from a drawer in the van, he sliced a decent rectangle from the side of the bucket, whereupon he put the bucket on his head, the rim of which settled neatly upon his shoulders. He'd guessed well: the hole allowed him to see out. He chuckled. Legal wigs were so yesterday, he decided. Ned Kelly hats were in. He donned the bucket and returned to the clearing.

Mia and Karl considered Lennie's headwear with puzzled looks. Mia said, "Hat for rain keeping off?"

Rawcus let loose a grey stream of excrement from his high branch, spattering Lennie's helmet.

"Australia is funny place," said Mia, shaking her head.

Karl looked up. Rawcus's bottom hovered above him. Karl shuffled along the log. Rawcus followed along his branch. Karl shuffled away. Rawcus followed. Karl gave in. He seemed to concede that worse things had happened to his bald head today.

Joe, binding Robbie's ankles to the chair legs, fought the urge to tell Lennie he looked like an idiot. Joe figured a more surgical approach was required. He went to the van and returned with one of the dust masks they used when cutting brickwork to insert electrical wiring in walls. He also carried a pair of electrically insulated, black rubber gloves, and the box cutter.

Lennie nodded at Joe's suggested costume change. He removed the bucket, put on the mask and gloves, and cut the air with the blade in smooth loops and turns. "If I sense unwillingness to cooperate in the accused, brain surgery may be required."

Robbie fought his restraints. "This is fucking madness!"

"You, Robbie, have an annoying habit of repeating ideas," said Lennie.

Joe opened the petrol can and splashed fuel on Mia's woodpile. He lit a match and flicked it into the pyramid.

"Whoa!" cried Rawcus from his branch above the court-room.

The percussive roar and whip of flames shocked Robbie so much he fell backward into the dirt. Joe hoisted him and his chair back up to sitting.

Joe plonked the upturned milk crate on the court line between Robbie and the log. Joe had a big bum to cushion the crisscrossed moulding on the crate's bottom, but it had him stuffed as to why all those bearded hipsters who lived near their home in the city fell over each other to sit on the damn things at the organic café up the street.

*

Night had fallen. The fire crackled. Lennie paced gripping the box cutter with his gloved hands held behind his back. He breathed hotly through the paper mask and said, "Robert Peter Hogg...how do you plead?"

"To what?" Robbie cried.

"Abduction, a smorgasbord of assault, armed robbery, accessory to rape ... I have little doubt you were planning to go next. So let's upgrade that to *intention to rape*."

Robbie saw an opening. "You can't convict someone for *intent*."

"I don't think you have been keeping up with the evolution of anti-terrorism laws."

Joe poked the fire with a stick. "May I ask the accused a question?"

"Fire away," said Lennie.

"How long have you been a copper, Robbie?"

"Years."

"See, Robbie," said Joe. "I'm as thick as a brick. My old headmaster, Mr Darian used to tell me this all the time. Anyway, I'm doing reading and writing classes these days. And I just happened to have a peek at the label inside your shirt when you fell over chasing freedom."

Robbie tried to stand but his chair restraints won the battle. An odour like rotten eggs wafted across the courtroom.

Joe continued. "Do you know what it said?"

Robbie stayed mute.

Lennie leaned eye-to-eye with the accused and posed another question: "Cat got your tongue?"

Robbie stayed mute.

Joe resumed. "That label said *Betty's Costume Hire*. I know that place. It's in the city in Darlinghurst. Very popular during the Christmas party season and Mardi Gras."

Lennie appeared gobsmacked. "Oh, my God! Robbie, are you one of those strip-o-gram sorts of cops?"

Robbie's face reddened as if his skull was an over-heating pressure cooker. Words seemed to smash their way out of his mouth: "Killing policemen will land you retards in the fires of hell!"

Lennie fingered his brow as if his skull was made of rubber and he was massaging his brain, trying to squeeze out thoughts. He snatched the air as if he had captured one. "I believe I have it! The accused will benefit by examining himself through an alternative reality. Will you do the honours please, Mr Bailiff?"

Joe smiled; he was not persuaded by the idea of *alternative reality*. That was Lennie's special subject. Joe reckoned there was just one reality, but it did get misshapen now and then. It was like denting your car on a power pole: you could try to panel beat it out if you wanted to, say by seeing a head-shrinker. Or you could live with it. Joe lived with his dents.

Joe opened the petrol can and extracted the baby-elephant-trunk nozzle which was normally used to pour the contents into the tanks of lawnmowers and other small machines.

Joe did Robbie the kindness of wiping the nozzle a couple of times on his board shorts. He grabbed the man's jaw with one hand, squeezing on its hinges until his mouth opened enough for him to get the nozzle's tip behind his front teeth.

Lennie said, "What do you think would happen, Robbie, if we filled your gullet with petrol and dropped a match in your mouth?"

Robbie bucked wildly. Joe held the nozzle firmly in place. "What do you reckon, Joe?"

Joe shook his head sagely. "We might start a bushfire. Remember last time?"

"Caused the local fire brigade a bucket load of grief," said Lennie. "So let's hold fire on that idea. But we'll keep it as an option."

Lennie turned to Mia. "Could you please pass the truth serum?"

She handed Lennie the fresh ether bottle. He flipped the cap and poured into the funnel, trying unsuccessfully to avoid spills and limit waste, as well as Robbie's gagging. They got about half a bottle into the accused. Joe extracted the nozzle.

Mia said seriously, "We have bad police in Poland too."

Karl put the discarded Ned Kelly bucket on his head. Rawcus patrolled the branch above.

*

"OK, Robbie," said Lennie, swishing his cutter to make an X, hoping a dash of scene-setting would accelerate an out-pouring of facts, now that the blue light had been given time to infiltrate the accused's synapses. "We are going to ask you questions. If we are not persuaded by the answers, we are going to dig some out with brain surgery. And – or – we will connect electrical leads between our car battery and your skull and promote a little mental stimulation. What do you call it, Joe?"

"Shock therapy."

Robbie's head tilted back and he looked straight up into a branch, flickering with shadows from the flames of the fire, upon which Rawcus stood. The bird leaned over and peered down upon the man.

"Is that you, Arty?" said Robbie.

"Arr-tee!" screeched Rawcus.

Joe flashed a thumbs-up at Lennie, who nodded.

While Robbie made eyes with Rawcus, Joe stepped behind the tree trunk. Rawcus picked up the shift in the play and hopped inwards along the branch, climbing over limbs that took him behind the trunk so he could keep an eye on Joe.

A deep voice seemed to come from the tree. "Tell them our story, Robbie."

Mia grinned. Karl removed the bucket hat. Lennie sat on the milk crate with a look on his face like a fascinated kid in the front row of a pantomime. He wondered if Joe had been inspired by the talking trees in *The Lord of the Rings* movies they had watched last weekend for the umpteenth time. Lennie took his phone out of his pocket and pressed some buttons; the campfire and a half-moon made excellent mood light as he started video recording.

"Is that really you, Arty?" said Robbie, his eyes circling the tree, apparently searching for clues.

Lennie sniggered. If this man was putting on an act, it was pretty good. But so was the ether.

"It's my spirit," said the tree. "Tell these people our true story and our souls will be washed of sin."

Lennie observed Mia and Karl: they looked more like a giant possum and an orangutan than a couple of recently traumatised backpackers.

Robbie asked for another sip of the blue spirit, and a cigarette from the pack in his top pocket. Lennie cut the bindings on his hands to let him drink and smoke – and Robbie talked as the fire crackled and its orange and blue plumes snaked skyward.

Robbie explained that he and Arty had come up with a brilliant idea: they purchased an old police paddy wagon from a government auction, that was stripped of its police insignia of course. But Arty was a commercial signwriter by trade. And Robbie owned a rural property upon which there was a workshop, and inside the workshop, they had secreted their second-hand wagon, re-painted and re-stickered it with blue-and-white checkerboard, and printed the words *Police* in all the right places.

At 3am one freezing mid-winter morning, when no other living creature was mad enough to be outside, they had crow-barred a panel of red, white, and blue lights from the rooftop of a real police car.

"Cocky coppers," Robbie sniggered. "Their bright lights weren't even alarmed!"

He laughed harder about how easy it was to use his phone to take pictures of the parked paddy wagon and use it as a re-construction template. Then Robbie had the equally brilliant idea to steal some police uniforms from *Betty's Costume Hire*. They bought their police-style utility belts online from China via eBay, along with replica Tasers. Their pistols were real and came from a crystal-meth dealer in the city. It was Robbie's idea to smoke ice, and drive the country roads looking for tourists to terrify and rob. It was the most fun they'd had in their lives. They'd been doing it for weeks. They'd even fooled some real coppers in the main street of nearby Redcliffe Valley who waved at them as if they were birds of a feather passing in the night.

"I mean," said Robbie, chuckling at his wit, "what copper ever suspects that another copper is not a copper?"

As for the Polish chick...well, Robbie said with a philosophical shrug, she just happened to be unlucky, or lucky depending on how you looked at it, when Arty got horny after a few meth pipes. And her boyfriend? Mr Chemo-skull with his stupid showbiz wig? Well, he should have shut his trap and taken things on the chin. But oh, no. He had to play the hero. And now? The girl was going to jail for life for driving the tomahawk through Arty's skull.

"Can I have some more of that petrol?" said Robbie.

"Nup," said Lennie.

Having obtained by Lennie's reckoning enough evidence to burn the man at a stake, depending on the historical era and the laws in the State where the offence was put to trial, he turned off his video recorder and said, "Robbie, this is the end."

"Of the bottle?"

"Of you," said Lennie, as Joe stepped out from behind the tree.

"Please. I have a family."

"C'est la vie," said Lennie. "Now, I'd like to summarise...It's true that Mia sunk the hawk into Arty's scone. But the provocation was extreme. It was a crime of passion in a reversed sort of way. She was not of right mind at the time, due to the actions of you and Arty.

"Now you, Robbie, are a confessed, terrible fraud. A perpetrator of violent crimes on the innocent, and a willing accessory to other crimes – as my video recording will attest. Edited version for social media purposes, and another for the real police, of course."

Lennie waved his phone and continued, "Joe, will you keep an eye on Robbie while I have a conference with Mia and Karl?"

The trio huddled and talked in low voices. They returned to centre court.

Lennie said to Robbie, "Here's the deal. Your fingerprints are all over the murder weapon. In a nutshell, you can rise out of that chair and put Arty in the back of your paddy wagon. Then you get behind the wheel, drive back to your work-shop or wherever you like, dispose of the body, and junk the vehicle. Arty becomes another missing person. You will have a few nightmares now and then. End of story."

Robbie gazed wide-eyed and gape-mouthed at Lennie.

"Alternatively," said Lennie, "you can kick up a stink and suffer worse nightmares more often...How could that be, you're thinking? For a start, we have four witnesses here who saw you kill your mate in a drug-fuelled craze after you bushwhacked us, and Arty raped Mia while you held us at gunpoint. You got cranky because you couldn't get it up. As I said, your prints are on that hawk. Oh, and don't forget the digital copy of your confession."

Robbie huffed and puffed. The fire crackled.

Lennie cut an X in the air. "Time's up."

Robbie sighed. "Arty *was* an orphan...and he had a lot of debts, so when I think about it, he could have done a runner. I'll take option one."

"Excellent choice," said Lennie, baulking at his choice of words, realising he was channelling the host of a TV game show he'd been forced to watch in prison by two giant Samoans. Some scars last for life, he thought, though on a happier note the Samoans were now dead. Problem was, the departed Enoka brothers had three large, live siblings floating around and they were none too fond of Lennie. In fact, Lennie had the sixth sense this evening that they were close by.

Robbie rolled Arty up in the canvas tarp, dragged him into the back of the paddy wagon, and drove away.

While Mia and Karl tidied their campervan, Lennie and Joe doused the fire from a water carrier, scattered the ashes, and dusted over the courtroom floor with leafy branches until it looked pretty much like every other part of the track.

"Where's that leftover bottle of ether, the one we used at trial?" Lennie asked Joe, who shook his head to say he had no idea.

Lennie grumbled as he peeled the rubber gloves off his hands. "Robbie! That thieving little prick...let's get out of here."

"Look at him," said Joe affectionately, pointing at Rawcus who was sleeping on the branch above the sitting-log, whimpering now and then as if he was dreaming. "Posing as a proper bird."

Joe picked up a long stick and roused Rawcus who was not happy and went beak and claw after Joe who fended him off long enough to pour some bird tranquilisers, otherwise known as pumpkin seeds dusted with Valerian herb, into his tuna tin. Mia and Karl swapped phone numbers and email addresses with Lennie. Mia gave Lennie a hip flask of blue light as a parting gift.

The contortionists climbed into their campervan and followed the Firefly to the main bitumen road where they parted ways. The Firefly circled back into the bush. There was unfinished business at the end of the track...

PART 2 - DOUBLE CROSS

1 - FOUNTAIN OF YOUTH

Three weeks earlier, around midday...

JOE MOTORED the Firefly through the peaks and troughs of a treacherous mountain trail. Lennie and Rawcus rode the bumps wide-eyed beside him. Joe stopped beside a tree outside *No1, The End of the World*.

Nailed to the tree's trunk was a battered metal sign painted with orange letters on a blue background: *Private Property – Keep Out*. Beside the sign was a steel-mesh road gate. The chain that kept it locked was cut. The gate was open.

Joe accelerated onto a horseshoe-shaped driveway, pulling up in a clearing carved from dense forest. A corrugated-iron-clad shed flecked with rust stood alone. At one end of the shoebox-shaped building, the roller door was up.

"Uh, oh!" squawked Rawcus.

On the long side of the shed, protected by a metal awning over a concrete veranda, a single wooden door was swinging open.

"Maybe this *Fountain of Youth* thing isn't meant to happen," said Joe, who killed the engine.

"Maybe we need to improve our security," growled Lennie, inside whose head a blueprint was forming for a medieval contraption.

Rawcus shook his head and climbed onto Joe's shoulder.

Upon external inspection of the shed, the trio discovered that a hole, which looked hardly big enough for a dog to crawl through, had been cut in the roller door with a metal-grinder. Internal examination revealed that the invaders had left multiple and variously-sized boot prints, including what appeared to be a child's footprints.

Lennie and Joe, having more than academic knowledge of the art of break-and-enter, concluded that a kid, or a very small adult, had been sent through the hole as a front-runner to unlock the inside floor bolts and push the roller up. The thieves had then stolen a load of very expensive hydroponic gardening equipment, and destroyed an experimental crop that Joe and Lennie had codenamed FOY, for the *Fountain of Youth*...

*

The chemist, or TC as they nicknamed him, had persuaded Lennie and Joe to join him in the FOY project months ago. TC was a botanical expert with university qualifications and at the initial planning meeting he had described his idea as an "avant-garde venture into genetic modification".

TC continued, "There's a native plant called *erythroxylum*. It's a stimulant that's propagating in the wild all around *The*

End. Now, I've worked out that if you can hybrid it with a plant from Easter Island called *schoenoplectus californicus*, or Totora in layman's speak, we can create a super-compound that stimulates the human body to produce molecules called *nicotinamide adenine dinucleotide*.

"Bin the show pony banter, will you mate?" Lennie had replied. "Stick to plain English. Short words packed with power, not chatter that locks blokes like us out of understanding. OK? And we'll all get along fine."

"OK," TC said. "Let's call this *nicotinamide adenine dinucleotide*, NAD for short. Yes?"

"Good. NAD."

"NAD is the fountain of youth, Lennie. In the lab, I've worked with mice who were the human equivalent of sixty years of age. We upped their NAD levels, and a week later it's like they were twenty. It even dissolved cancerous tumours."

TC explained that like human creation, NAD could be produced by mating two parent plants. TC reckoned he'd come up with a "1+1 = 5 genetic cocktail". Or in plain English, a "super child".

"Heard of a bloke named Adolf Hitler?" Lennie said.

TC sighed. "I'm not proposing we exterminate people and replace them with a master race. Think of taking NAD like time travel, where you keep your memories but your body goes back to its peak condition."

Lennie had considered TC's proposition and decided to give it a shot, especially because it might kill the big C which had chewed up a few of his friends. Joe thought it was a loonie plot fit for a sci-fi movie, but he was keen to learn some new hydroponic gardening techniques.

Secrecy in development was critical because TC trusted none of his scientific colleagues back in the city in the corporate and academic worlds. TC reckoned if the big end of town cracked the large-scale chemistry of NAD first, they'd whip it off into some gated community where rich people got it first and greedied on it for generations before any regular people got a taste, if ever. TC had argued, "If we don't do it, someone else will and they may not be nice."

The FOY team and their secret project had been getting along fine, until the robbers nicked their high-powered fluorescent lights, humidifiers, and air-conditioning units. They also thieved solar panels and a back-up diesel generator that made electricity to keep the operation going off-the-grid without attracting the attention of the authorities, plus camp beds, folding chairs, a portable barbeque, gas bottles, and a snake-bite, first-aid kit which was pretty important given the place was thick with the beasts in the spring and summer, which was getting longer and hotter every year.

Pre-burglary, Lennie reckoned he and Joe could have survived a nuclear autumn at *The End of the World*. Though he conceded that a nuclear winter may have done them in. But now, with all their best kit gone, he reckoned they'd be lucky to last a few days of any of the four seasons of an apocalypse, which really pissed him off.

The most infuriating thing from Joe's point of view was that the galoots who trashed the shed had hurled onto the driveway the two dozen FOY plants that had been growing happily on metal frames with their roots dangling in troughs of liquid nutrients and pebbles, while their leaves floated in carefully incubated air behind a curtain of thick plastic sheets. It was a mindless slaughter of lives that had barely begun.

*

On surveying the trashing of the shed, Joe had noticed a fury growing in Lennie's eyes. It began with lightning flashes in the black space inside his blue irises, before the capillaries in the surrounding whites glowed like streams of fire. Joe knew Lennie's inner inferno would burn itself out eventually – as all the others he had witnessed had done – but what damage it might wreak on its journey from high-flame to ash had always been impossible for Joe to predict in much detail, despite them having been friends since they were kids.

As Joe had inspected the dead and dying plants on the crash site of the driveway searching for survivors, Lennie had leaped behind the wheel of the Firefly and demanded the keys from Joe. This action put Joe in an unusual position.

It wasn't that Joe wasn't up for a freewheeling adventure with Lennie, who was a licensed electrician by trade and the registered owner of the van that bore the words *Firefly Electrics* painted in red and black letters with a lightning bolt logo on its outside. The unusualness of Joe's position was that Lennie didn't drive very often because he had decided long ago "to put public peace and safety ahead of the pleasure I derive from the G-forces of my own acceleration."

Joe knew this was code for road rage and he admired his friend for making this sacrifice. But all things considered, it was a pretty good result because being in Lennie's passenger seat was as much fun as eating sand and cement. So Joe had become the primary vehicle driver in their partnership because in traffic he was as cool as a cucumber and hardly ever attracted the police or even got speeding fines from road cameras.

On Discovery Day, as Lennie dubbed the break-in event, Joe had simply taken a deep breath and tightened his seat-belt as Lennie catapulted the van out of the gates and shot along the curling, rising, falling dirt track, heading for the T-junction turn-off to a bitumen road that led to the nearest town of Redcliffe Valley.

"Branigan's workshop," Lennie had yelled, giving Joe the only clue to their destination.

The ride quickly threw Rawcus from his rod to the floor, whereupon he tumbled into the back of the van. Metal drawers had rained upon him after they slipped from their wall-mounted frames in the gravitational chaos. As Rawcus ducked and weaved from the bombardment, there was little comfort Joe could offer. He simply called to the bird: "Hang in there, mate."

Rawcus took Joe's advice, and about an hour later the brain-rattled trio were locked in the bowels of a shed owned by Dan Branigan, Redcliffe Valley's best motor mechanic, according to a billboard leading into town. Branigan was also a scrap metal dealer and re-seller of items for which "cash-only" was accepted, according to a sign in his office window. Lennie and Joe knew that Branigan was also inclined to the old-fashioned barter system of trading goods-for-goods which, like cash, avoided the need for messy paperwork trails.

"I have a plan," Lennie told Branigan. "It's up here," Lennie added, tapping a finger upon his skull.

Joe and Rawcus had watched as Lennie and Branigan welded together a steel cross cobbled together from old bed frames. It was just large enough to fix a human upon it – *if* you had wanted to fix one to it, Lennie had explained, keen to give Branigan the impression he was creating a work of art rather than a security device which was unlikely to pass government health and safety regulations.

Welded on one side of the cross's frame, on both the vertical and horizontal struts, were 13 sharpened spikes, each about the length of a human foot. Lennie had no time for even numbers, so the odd number of spikes was mission-critical. He and Branigan completed their sculpture by welding an O-ring to the skyward tip of the vertical bar of the cross.

"What's this for?" Branigan dared to ask as the last sparks flew.

Lennie had responded by going to the Firefly and returning with a kilo bag of Mars Grass which he tossed to the mechanic and said, "Remember what curiosity did to the cat."

"Whoof," Branigan barked, and packed some of the grass into a Sherlock Holmes pipe.

Lennie reckoned their finished product looked like a crucifixion cross that had mated with a giant, balding echidna.

Joe reckoned Lennie had lost the plot, but he'd been on many plot-free adventures with his friend and was not bailing out on this one.

Arriving back at the shed, Lennie had taken a reel of heavy-duty, nylon fishing line from a box in the back of the Firefly and worn it like a bracelet. He and Joe carried the cross to the shed and placed it spikes-up on the veranda. They opened the wooden side-door and swung it back against the veranda wall. Using a combination of brackets, screws, and bolts, they fixed the cross by the O-ring to the mid-point of the upper door-frame. The net effect was that the cross swung smoothly in and out of the shed, spikes facing outwards, with its tail just shy of the floor. Lennie bracketed and screwed a box cutter blade to the doorframe just above the lock housing.

Lennie used a ladder for the finishing touch: he anchored a steel loop to the ceiling of the shed, and got Joe to use a broom to push the tail of the cross up to him, whereupon Lennie attached the tail to the hook using the fishing line. He threw the reel to Joe.

"Hold it tight," Lennie said. "And don't stand in the door-frame in case this line snaps."

"Thanks for the tip," said Joe, who had no intention of being impaled on any one of 13 spikes.

Rawcus hopped from Joe's shoulder onto his head. "This won't end well!" he cried, parroting one of Aunty D's favour-ite phrases.

Lennie ignored the negativity, climbed down, and took the tense line from Joe. "Can you guys step outside? And push the door closed thanks."

Inside the shed, Lennie looped the fishing line around the door handle so that when the door was pulled open from outside, the line would be severed by the box cutter blade. That was the theory, anyway.

"Open Sesame!" Lennie yelled.

Joe pulled the door open and hurled himself and Rawcus sideways. The fishing line snapped and the tail of the cross slipped from the ceiling; the spiked beast flashed down with great ferocity.

"Ooh. That'll hurt," said Lennie, watching the cross swish back and forth through the doorframe with diminishing power.

They closed the door and re-set the cross, then patched the hole in the roller door with a scrap of rippled tin fixed on with rivets. They vacated via the roller door, securing it from the outside with new floor bolts slotted into the concrete slab and padlocked in place.

As they stepped towards the Firefly, Lennie said to Joe with a parental tone, "Just make sure you don't turn up here rat-faced and forget."

Rawcus shook his head. "Don't turn up here rat-faced!"

Joe wasn't troubled by that possibility, but he was troubled. He asked Lennie if he could do him a favour and write the words *Danger – Do Not Enter* on the outside of the wooden door.

"I hate thieves too," Joe explained. "But a warning might be fair – before we make a kebab out of someone."

"Fair enough," conceded Lennie, whose anger at the break-in was waning with the passage of time and the therapeutic value of making sculpture, or art, or whatever head-shrinkers call it. "But as I learned in Cell Block E, when a couple of blokes jump you in the shower, there's not much point saying, *Please don't.*"

Joe knew that Lennie's prison stay had given him plenty of take-home memories, but Joe stuck to his guns. "I'm not asking you to write, *Please* Do Not Enter."

Lennie smiled, collected a red felt-tipped pen from the Firefly's glovebox, and wrote the warning, in not too big letters, on the door. But as he put the 'r' on Enter, he chuckled at life's ironies: the warning sign may actually work as a red rag to a stupid bull by suggesting there was something behind the door worth stealing, when in fact the shed was now virtually empty of anything but air, of which you could get all you want for free.

"What's so funny?" said Joe, as they stepped towards the Firefly.

"Too much thinking, not enough drinking."

They chain-locked the gate, snapped open cold beers, and headed for the city.

2 - PAGO

Tonight...

AFTER leaving Mia and Karl on the main road with directions to Sydney, and advice for the contortionists to leave
Australia swiftly but without eye-catching haste, lest Robbie
should change his mind about Arty's disappearing act, or he
should stuff up the clean-up operation as the ether wore off
and his mental abilities shrank back to normal – Joe motored
through mottled moonlight on the track towards *The End of
the World*.

"Phew!" Lennie sniffed through his open window as they
closed in on their destination. "Smell that?"

"I thought it was Rawcus," said Joe.

Rawcus, standing on his rod, eyed Joe indignantly.

The gate was chain-locked when they arrived. And the
Private Property – Keep Out sign was intact.

Lennie hopped out and unlocked the gate. Joe drove
through and turned onto the horseshoe-shaped driveway. As
Lennie was chaining the gate back to the post, the Firefly's
horn honked a distress code. Lennie ran towards the alarm.

In the brilliance of the van's headlights, a plump figure stood in the side-doorway of the shed.

Joe jumped from the van, leaving the engine running and lights on, and joined Lennie to examine the work of the steel cross.

It was near midnight and the air was cool, but flies fizzed angrily about the corpse as Joe and Lennie zeroed in. The men used their fingers to pinch their noses.

A sliver of headlight lit a dark tattoo on the fat neck of the bald-headed deceased, who was dressed in a sloppy grey tracksuit and brilliant white training shoes.

"Abracadabra?" said Joe, who despite winning an award last week at his adult literacy class was having trouble deciphering the tatt on the folds of flesh. "Some sort of magic spell?"

"Na," Lennie replied. "Seen it in prison. *Allahu Akbar.* Mussie language. Translates as *God is Great.*"

Joe moved to the side of the impalee. "Uh, oh. I recognise that face. Or what's left of it."

Lennie took a squiz. "Shit. That face could always scare bark off trees."

Joe said, "So what would Pago Enoka be doing opening doors out here? ...Mate?"

Lennie was peering into the distant night sky. "Out there," he said, pointing. "See those lights? Is that a spaceship?"

Joe looked up, guessing the Polish elixir was still working its way out of Lennie's brain. "Probably a satellite. Or a plane."

Lennie wasn't persuaded, but he swung his gaze back to earth and Pago's head.

Joe swished a hand at a squadron of flies that had decided Joe's eyes were a tasty side-dish to their main feast of splintered skull. Still pinching his nose, he squatted and picked a pencil-sized stick off the ground.

Positioning himself so he didn't create shadows from the Firefly's headlights, Joe poked Pago like he'd seen detectives do on old TV shows when they examined bodies at crime scenes. Joe concluded that a spike had penetrated Pago's left eye because a steel nib was jutting from the back of his skull behind the spot where he calculated the eye socket would be. There was also reasonable evidence that another spike had pierced Pago's throat: a tip was poking from the back of his neck. The mathematically precise spacing of the spikes by Lennie during the cross's construction suggested third, fourth, and fifth spears had entered Pago's torso – but Pago's belly was so large that those tips were not visible.

Rigor mortis was a term Joe had learned from TV docos about chemical changes in dead bodies. He concluded this condition was doing little to hold Pago upright. The changes only stiffen a body for a day or two after death, and Joe reasoned that the buckled lintel of the metal doorframe, to which the cross's O-ring was hooked, was doing most of the heavy lifting.

Lennie pointed at the words *Danger – Do Not Enter* that he had scratched on the door with a felt pen. "Couldn't he read?"

"Not all of us can."

Lennie nodded. "Should've drawn a skull and crossbones, is that what you're saying?" He backed away from the smell, released the finger-pinch on his nose, and recalled his original concern that writing the danger sign might actually work as a red rag to a stupid bull. "Wonder why he came?"

"There's a prime suspect," said Joe, who moved away too, released his nostrils, and tossed the stick.

Lennie nodded. "The Chemist."

"He's the weak link," Joe agreed.

Lennie sighed. "What a day. I'm knackered. Now we've got to dig a very big hole."

"I'll get the pick and shovel," said Joe.

"Bring some gloves too mate. And a couple of tranquilisers."

Lennie studied Pago. The difference between life and death was so much about time and place, and the company you keep. Just yesterday, a speeding bus had whizzed within a whisker of splattering Lennie when he tripped off a kerb in the city. Joe had grabbed him back from extinction, or possibly lifelong vegetative paralysis, by the shirt collar. Maybe it had been Pago's fate, thought Lennie, to depart this mortal coil on a spiked cross from the day he was born. Weirdest thing was, he and Joe had made this trip to take the bloody cross down before some knucklehead stepped into it!

Joe opened the sliding door of the van and gave Rawcus advice. "Best you grab a nap, mate. It's ugly out there."

Rawcus, balancing with one foot on his rod as if practicing tai chi, fluffed his feathers. "Ugly out there!" the bird cried.

"Nap time, mate." Joe popped the black sleeping beanie over Rawcus's head.

Joe returned to Lennie with the pick and shovel slung over one shoulder, two pairs of leather gloves stuffed into his shorts' waistband, clutching two icy cold beer cans in his spare hand.

He and Lennie retreated further to the upwind side of Pago where the stink and flies didn't bother them as much.

"Listen, mate," said Lennie, snapping the cap on a can. "That sign on our gate says *Private Property – Keep Out*. And busting through someone's door uninvited is the same as busting through their butthole."

Joe raised his eyebrows.

"My point is," Lennie explained, "if you're going to cross another person's threshold, against their wishes and with bad intent in your heart, it's rape. You can use any legal lingo you like. And rapists deserve to be hoist by their own petard."

"Can you try that in plain English, mate?" Joe swigged his beer.

Lennie had recalled the *hoist petard* stuff from a pub quiz night he'd attended with his aunt and her friends who were trivia gurus. They'd explained, in answer to a question from the quizmaster, that a bloke named Shakespeare had thrown the phrase into a play named Hamlet, and it meant that a bomb-maker is blown up by his own bomb in an act of poetic justice. This idea tickled Lennie's fancy as much as the Buddhist notion of karma.

Lennie paraphrased for Joe. "Pago fucked himself."

"That's one way of putting it," said Joe. "Sun'll be up in a few hours. Best we get crackin' under the cover of darkness. Who knows who might turn up on the track after those fake coppers have been runnin' around?" He pointed to the edge of the forest.

"Agreed," said Lennie. "That's a decent anti-haunting distance given the circumstances. We don't want to give Pago's dodgy spirit an easy shot at taking up residence in the shed."

"We really should burn him," said Joe. "But that could take a day or so."

Lennie looked thoughtful. "Muslims don't do cremation. They go straight in the ground. Not even a coffin."

"Pago's as much a real Mussie as we are Brides of Christ," said Joe, who drained his beer.

"True," Lennie replied. "But did I tell you that his mother is a witch doctor? They call it *FoFo* it in the Pacific Islands, a voodoo thing. Let's hope she hasn't got some magic that keeps track of her boys."

"If she's got that sort of radar, it didn't work for Jona and Toku, did it?" Joe crushed his empty can. "I mean, a farmer's dog found their bodies by that dam, not their mum."

"Good point," said Lennie. "We better bury Pago so deep that paws won't find him either."

Joe lobbed his can into a recycling box on the veranda and took from his shorts pocket a near-empty softpack of tobacco cigarettes.

"Here," he said, passing a fresh cancer stick to Lennie.

Lennie snapped it in half and stuffed the pieces in each of his nostrils. Joe bent an entire stick and stuffed the whole

V into one of his bugle-sized holes, then filled his second the same way.

While Lennie and Joe were unsure about the ripple effect this unwanted visitor was going to have on their lives, they were sure about one thing: *No 1, The End of the World* was the right address for them to be able to deal with this situation with a minimum of fuss. At least Joe was sure.

In the distant sky, Lennie watched alien lights circling, beaming down and scanning the earth. Something coughed inside the forest...

3 - LORD OF THE FLIES

"DID YOU HEAR THAT?" Lennie cupped a hand behind an ear and aimed the improvised sound-catcher at the trees.

"Just a roo," Joe replied with a clogged-nose twang. He pulled a ciggie from a nostril to be clear: "Let's get Pago off this cross."

Lennie knew kangaroos barked and that their barks could sound like human's coughing. But he also knew that Joe's ears had taken a few mean hits when he was a kid and his eardrums were scarred. Right now, Lennie would swear on Aunty D's grave that he'd heard the bronchial rattle of a smoker's cough in the bush. He listened. Silence.

Joe plugged the de-stinker back in his nostril and stepped to Pago's right side. The flies shimmied in angry waves around the Easter Island statue-like head. Lennie stepped to the left side.

"So now there's just two of the five brothers left," mused Joe, pulling on his gloves.

"Pago was third in line to the throne," added Lennie, stroking the tip of his right ear where a chunk was missing due to an accident in the Silverwater Prison metalwork shop a couple of years ago.

Toku, the second born of the Samoan siblings, had clamped a pair of pliers to Lennie's ear and torn away some flesh. Lennie had brought the ear remodelling upon himself, the eldest brother, Jona, explained, by selfishly declining a job offer to become a domestic and international drug courier for the Enokas when he departed the jail for civilian life.

Unfortunately for the Enoka family, Jona and Toku died about a year ago from what the authorities called "misadventure" while on the run from the Australian Federal Police, who suspected the two brothers were selling drugs to raise money for branches of Islamic State which had clung on to life in North Africa and South-East Asia after the caliphate was largely rooted out of Syria and Iraq. Following the brothers' deaths, Lennie and Joe had been sleeping well, hoping that neither the handtools nor shadows of an Enoka would touch them again.

"Ready?" said Joe, who gripped Pago's right wrist, then inserted his other hand into the crevice of Pago's cavernous armpit. Lennie mirrored Joe's moves.

"On the count of three," said Joe. "One, two..."

And they ripped Pago's body off the spikes.

"Oh, fuuck," moaned Lennie, as he and Joe lost their hold on Pago's torso which thudded onto the dirt by the veranda, spilling glistening sausages. Pago's head remained stuck on the spike.

"One sec," said Joe, who grabbed a wrist-thick, tree branch from the ground nearby. "Stand back."

Joe dug the end of the branch between Pago's face and the cross and levered. With a slurp, the head slid along the spike and rolled off the tip, landing on the concrete veranda with a dull crack. Flies chased their head.

"*Lord of the Flies*," muttered Lennie, recalling a novel he read when he was a teenager. The schoolboy protagonists' plane crashed on an island and plunged them into a world without adults. It started pretty well for the kids but took a nasty turn when they stuck a pig's head on a stick and called it *Lord of the Flies*.

"What are you on about?" said Joe.

"Do you ever feel like you're living inside a story?"

"I just feel like I'm living," said Joe. "We should have dug the hole first."

"Now you tell me," said Lennie. "What can we carry him in?"

"Well," said Joe. "Arty got our tarp. You gave Mia our blanket. So we're down to your sleeping bag."

"My Christmas present? Shit, can't we put his head in a shopping bag and drag the rest of him."

"We're out of bags. He's already split open. Sacrifices are called for."

They rolled Pago into the open-sided sleeping bag, added his head, and zipped it up. Joe turned the Firefly's engine off to save fuel, and cut the lights to save the battery. After all that sweat and toil, Joe cracked a fresh beer to share with Lennie.

Lennie carried the pick and shovel and a torch. Joe dragged the body bag with one hand, clutching the unfinished can with his spare. They chose a spot between towering trees. The night was so silent they could hear a lizard crawling among the leaf litter, or it may have been a snake; they weren't sure. They heard a cough.

They turned as one to the source. Lennie's torch lit a stranger's face.

4 - DARLING, I'M HOME!

A MAN was leaning against a tree trunk.

Lennie's torch beam slid up and down a stocky, dark-skinned figure with a rough grey beard and crewcut hair. He was wearing green overalls and black boots.

"Am I glad to see you guys?" the man said with a voicebox that sounded sandpapered. "I've been lost out here for days."

Ken explained that he'd been bushwalking alone. The trail had turned into an overgrown dead end and he'd lost his bearings. He'd been stumbling around, drinking from puddles and eating bush tucker like mushrooms and grubs.

"I'd kill for a cold beer," Ken said, nodding at Joe's.

"Only hotties left," said Joe.

"Good by me," said Ken. "I'd kill for a ciggie too."

Joe furrowed his brow. "Shall I run you a warm bath and whip up a chicken dinner too?"

"Ha," said Ken. "I don't eat white meat."

Joe pulled a broken cigarette from his nose. "Here."

Ken smiled. "Got a fresh one?"

Lennie nodded at Joe, who read his friend's *let's humour this turkey until we work out his game* expression. Joe stepped towards the Firefly to collect a beer.

Lennie studied Ken's giant grin: his face was not the cocktail of desperation and relief that Lennie believed was warranted for a bloke who'd been lost for days. In fact, Ken looked incredibly comfortable leaning against the tree, almost like he'd been waiting for visitors.

"Always go bushwalking in overalls?" said Lennie.

"Do you mind?" said Ken, holding his hand against the glare of Lennie's torch. Lennie turned the beam off and let the moonlight do its stuff.

"Ta," Ken said, staying in the shadows. "Oh, and the attire…I'd been working on a busted tractor for a farmer over the back of Redcliffe Valley. Staying there in fact. Thought I'd take a stroll after work. Bingo – it gets dark, and I'm lost."

"So you'd know the mechanic in Redcliffe," said Lennie. "A woman named Billy Bourke?"

"Na. I'm new here. Why I got lost, mate." Ken chuckled. "She got a nice set of spanners?"

"She has to deal with a lot of tools," said Lennie, an electric feeling whizzing up and down his spine. Lennie wondered if he should grab the handle of his pick and drive one of its steel beaks into Ken's foot, or earhole. Joe returned with the beer, pulled a ciggie from his pocket, and handed them to Ken.

The beer foamed as Ken gulped. He wiped his lips on his sleeve and said, "What's in the sleeping bag?"

"A dead body," said Lennie, with the straightest face he could muster. He took a cigarette lighter from his jeans pocket and lit Ken's smoke.

"Ta," said Ken, puffing hungrily. "I was guessing treasure. Gold, wads of banknotes. Tasty drugs. This'd be a good place to stash stuff. Am I right, or am I right?"

Joe said, "Listen, Ken. Our dog got bitten by a snake. So we have to dig a hole."

"Must have been a big bugger."

"An eastern brown," said Joe. "Went at him like an angry bullwhip."

"I meant the dog."

"He was a Great Dane," said Lennie. "With a lot of toys to take to doggie heaven."

Ken dragged on his smoke and smiled. "Are you guys heading back to civilisation at some point? Because I'd love a ride into town."

"No problem, Ken," said Lennie. "You take your beer and have a seat on the veranda over there. And when me, and me mate, are finished burying poor old *Rhino* here, we'll whip you into town."

Ken shuffled towards the shed.

"Fuck!" Joe hissed. "He'll see the bloody cross."

"He's already seen us stuffing Pago into the bag. Remember that cough we heard before we pulled him off the spikes?"

"What are we going to do with him? I don't feel like killing a bloke for being a witness."

"He's making himself at home," said Lennie, pointing at the doorway of the shed.

Ken, with the cigarette dangling from his lips, was pushing the cross as casually as if he was pushing a kid in a swing, his other hand clutching his beer.

Ken looked back at them and pulled the ciggie from his mouth, just as a spike missed spearing his hip. "This is genius," he cried. "What a welcome mat for the happy household...*Darling, I'm home.*"

Joe sighed and grabbed the pick. He attacked the earth with fury, stopping after a few swings to dig out the loosened dirt with the shovel. Lennie looked skyward – the alien lights were back, and closer, sweeping the forest canopy.

"Mate," he said to Joe. "Let's drag Pago into the scrub. We're about to have more visitors."

Joe looked up. Spot beams swept the dark; an engine thrummed. Chuff-chuff-chuff.

Joe jumped from the shallow ditch and helped Lennie drag Pago into the undergrowth and toss fallen branches on him. As they stepped from under the trees into the clearing, searchlights blazed from the sky, hurting their eyes. Sirens whinnied, growing louder. Red, white and blue lights strobed through the trees coming from the direction of the track.

"Say cheese," Lennie called to Joe amid the escalating din of the helicopter blades. He waved at the chopper as if he was welcoming guests. "Either this is Ken's search party," he yelled. "Or Robbie has dobbed us in...Joe?"

Inside the doorway of the shed, Joe was standing at full stretch. He had an arm's length crowbar in one hand and was working from the inner shed, standing behind the spikes. He jammed the bar's beak into the brackets that fixed the

O-ring to the doorframe and wrenched and clawed. The cross crashed onto the veranda.

The chopper floated over the middle of the clearing, hurling dust and leaves that blurred the entire campsite. Through the whip-roar of the blades, a voice crackled from a loudspeaker: "Have you seen a man wearing green overalls? Wave if you have."

Lennie held his palms up as if hadn't heard the question.

Under the cover of the dust, Joe carried the cross onto the dirt at the side of the veranda and dropped it so the spikes penetrated the earth. He sat on the flat-backed centrepiece, trying to look relaxed on what he hoped to pass off as a designer garden seat, the sort of thing rich, trendy Christians might buy at Easter. If hipsters got away with milkcrate café seats, Joe thought, this item was a no-brainer.

Three police cars, flashing their chase lights, rumbled head-to-tail around the driveway and stopped side-by-side in the clearing near the Firefly. Armed officers wearing bullet-proof vests leaped from the doors.

Lennie put his hands up. Joe stood and did the same.

An officer stepped towards Lennie. "We are looking for a man named Ken Milan. He is about this height," he yelled, gesturing with a hand. "Short grey hair. Dark skin. He was last seen wearing green overalls."

"That is weird," said Lennie, who was looking at an object sitting in the dirt beside the open side-door of the Firefly: Ken's green overalls were discarded as if the man inside them had evaporated.

Lennie nodded at the pile of clothing. "That's what's left of your man."

"Do you know what he is wearing now?" said the officer, picking up the overalls.

"His undies?"

"Did you actually see that?"

"Give me a sec," said Lennie, who stepped into the back of the Firefly. Moments later he stepped out waving a few clear plastic wrappers. "The cheeky prick has stolen a brand new set of Firefly Electrics track pants, a hoodie, and a bloody baseball cap. This promotional stuff costs a fortune."

The officer's handheld radio crackled. The helicopter took flight, heading high and inland. A voice on the radio said a dark-clad figure had been spotted near a shack further up the track.

The officer talked into his radio. He turned to Lennie, "One of my colleagues will take a statement. Thanks for your help." He quickstepped towards his car.

Lennie called after him, "Who *is* this bloke?"

The officer yelled. "His name is Ken Milan. A serial killer. He did a farmer in last night, not far from here. I suggest you blokes talk to my colleagues, pack up and get out of here. Car doors locked."

5 - IS THAT YOU KENNY?

"THIS IS A VERY INTERESTING SEAT," said the police officer who took Lennie's and Joe's contact details and brief statements about their encounter with Ken Milan. "But it's uncomfortable."

"That's modern design for you, Geoff," said Lennie, as the officer wiggled his skinny bum on an even skinnier strut of the cross. "More form than function. It's a prototype I've been working on. I make a model first. I don't know this one will get to market."

"How long have you been a designer, Mr Larson?" the officer said.

"Since I was a child, I guess. I started making models of myself. They were so realistic that my gran would talk to them," said Lennie, neglecting to mention that the old lady was certified demented. Lennie shuffled sideways, hoping to keep Geoff's line-of-sight off one of Pago's eyeballs which had escaped his head and was staring at the copper from the dirt near Lennie's foot. Lennie stepped on it and smiled at Geoff.

The officer's radio crackled. Ken had disappeared into the heavily forested mountains to the north-west.

"How many people has he killed?" said Lennie.

"We think four. He's been on the run for about a year. He poses as a farm labourer and bush mechanic. Mostly. He's pretty good at disguises. And bushcraft. He claims to have aboriginal blood in him, but there is no evidence of that."

Lennie shook his head. "Now he's posing as an electrician, dressed in our clobber!"

"As the boss suggested," said Geoff. "You guys should pack up and get out of here until we catch this lunatic." His radio spluttered: a possible sighting of Ken. "Got to get back to the chase. We'll be in touch."

Geoff and his partner climbed into their patrol car and Lennie and Joe waved them off through the gates.

"Let's bury Pago and do as the boss says," Lennie concluded. "Eyes and ears peeled though. If Kenny has the balls to double back, he can join Pago in a hole. And in his undies too. That merchandise he nicked cost us a fortune."

Joe smiled. "Reckon he'll tell on us if they catch him?"

"It's a decent risk."

"We can't bury Pago here now," said Joe.

Lennie nodded. "We better take that cross too. Oh, and this bloody thing." He lifted his foot off the rogue eyeball; it stared at him.

They plugged their nostrils with fresh, broken cigarettes, dragged Pago's sleeping bag out of the forest, and loaded him in the back of the Firefly with the eye. They placed the spiked cross on top of him, points up out of respect. After locking the shed they drove out with Rawcus wobbling on his rod and rolling his head as if overcome by the fumes of decomposition.

"You thinking what I'm thinking?" said Joe.

"That he's hamming it up? A proper bush bird wouldn't get crook at the smell of rotten meat."

"Na. Not that. Blackhill Falls," said Joe. "The old asbestos mine is at the bottom of that cliff. Nobody's been near it for decades. And they won't be back there in our lifetime."

"Fear of lung cancer will do that to you," said Lennie, nodding approval at the new burial site nomination. He opened the glovebox, plucked out a pre-rolled joint of Mars Grass which he lit, puffed heartily, and passed to Joe.

After negotiating as many twists and turns as a pretzel, Joe drove onto a narrower trail and arrived at a dead end. He parked by a locked gate dressed with a sign: *Danger! Do Not Pass.* They strapped hiking headlamps onto their skulls.

After removing the steel cross, they hauled Pago's bagged body out of the van and dragged it under a wire-strand fence beside the gate. Joe pulled the bag. Lennie walked backward, using a leafy branch to dust their trail. Minutes later, they reached another sign: *Abandoned Asbestos Mine. Asbestos Kills. No Entry.*

"That's what'll kill you," said Lennie, his headlamp fathoming pathetically the sheer drop from the cliff's edge. "What do you reckon? Two hundred metres?"

Joe nodded. "The last time I looked down there in daylight there was a cave opening big enough to swallow a car."

"I feel a bit cruel," said Lennie, "tossing this trash down the gullet of poor old Mother Earth."

"Yeah," said Joe. "But on the upside, this sleeping bag I bought you is made of natural fibres. So it's not as if we're shoving a plastic bag down her throat."

"Guess so." Lennie brightened with a fresh thought. "And the contents are organic too."

They seesawed the bag between them and with perfect synchronicity launched it into space. They heard a hollow gulp.

"Bullseye, I reckon," said Joe.

Lennie wasn't as relaxed as Joe about leaving things to chance. So he put a hand in his jeans pocket and touched a little-finger sized piece of Bloodwood that he had carved and called a Lucky Jack.

Lennie had a collection of Jacks at home in a felt-lined box on his dressing table. He collected them like other people do watches. His Jacks had to be made of wood because wood was composed by nature, like water and lightning, flesh and bone, fruit and flowers. To be properly empowered, a Jack must first be dipped in seawater before drying in the sun. After that, a quick touch at least once every day provided low-cost insurance against life's risks: things like incurable pain, permanent madness, or being overcome by villains.

As they walked back from the cliff, they double-dusted their footprints with leafy branches. Lennie also swept over the Firefly's tyre tracks as Joe backed out to the main track. After driving for a while, they stopped and dumped the steel cross, spikes down, into a swamp, and watched it sink into the mud. As they were preparing to depart, they heard a cough...

"Is that you Kenny?" Lennie called into the bush, using his headlamp to light it.

Silence.

"Come out and have another beer and a ciggie," Lennie continued. "We're on your side, mate."

Silence.

He and Joe stepped back towards the van. Rawcus, who was patrolling the roof racks from where he had observed the cross-tossers at work, shuffled to the outer edge of the rack nearest to his approaching friends. The feathered mimic coughed, nice and crackly. The bird turned an eye downwards, appearing to enjoy the near-petrified looks on the faces of both men.

"Fuck you, Rawcus!" growled Lennie, as his heartrate geared down from Olympic sprinter to Sunday sleeper. "No beer for a week."

"Fuck you!" cried Rawcus, winking. "Fuck you!"

6 - NEURONS

JOE TURNED from the dirt track onto the bitumen road to Redcliffe Valley en route to the city. The Firefly's headlamps lit the black tar and the white dashes of the lane-markers flashed by.

Joe said, "I have a confession to make."

"I wish you wouldn't use that word," said Lennie, his face tinged blue under the glow of the dashboard lights.

"What word?"

"*Confession*. It gives me the heebie-jeebies. Can't you say something like *reveal*?"

"Sorry," said Joe. "Old habits."

Lennie appeared spellbound by the flickering road markers.

Joe shook his head. "The church, hey. Once it gets it claws in ya mind, it never lets go."

But Lennie wasn't listening anymore.

"Earth to Lennie," said Joe, "Earth to Lennie."

Lennie was in a trance. And as the silent minutes passed, Joe could not stop his own thoughts being pulled into what he believed was the same black hole that Lennie had spiralled into, a hole inside which their shared childhoods tumbled head-over-tail and where adult laughter roared...

*

Lennie and Joe had *the privilege*, they were told by a visiting black-robed Bishop, of being altar boys at Father Francesco's church which was located beside their school.

But not all altar boys were the same, Joe learned. Father Francesco told Joe that he was fat and smelly and reminded him of a "slug" as compared with "pretty" Lennie.

Joe's lack of access to regular clean clothes and fresh fruit and veggies was outside his control, him being a kid and reliant on adults, so Lennie explained at the time. But Joe learned to like being repulsive to adults. In fact, he worked on it. Because it meant he was never invited into Father Francesco's special tent overnight on Sunday school camping trips – like Lennie was.

Joe, however, had his own extra-curricular educational experiences. His were with their primary school's hairy-handed, stink-resistant headmaster, Mr Darian, who showed Joe imaginative things that could be done with an eel that lived in a fish tank in his office. Mr Darian gave Joe these lessons in detention after school. Joe only ever told one person who believed his stories about what happened with the water serpent. And that was Lennie. Joe tried to tell his mother the first time, but he learned that she preferred talking to her wine casks about life's mysteries.

These days, with him and Lennie grown up, it was a mystery to the police as to how Father Francesco disappeared from his house beside the church without leaving a trace of any kind. The police were equally perplexed as to how, about six months after the priest vanished, Mr Darian seemed to evaporate overnight from the bedroom in his beachside retirement home.

The missing men's friends and former colleagues, who Lennie and Joe bumped into occasionally at the bar at their local bowling club near the church and school, had asked them if they had any thoughts or feelings about the disappearances. Lennie and Joe could only scratch their heads in unison and offer echoed explanations such as, "UFO's...they were most likely taken by Unidentifed Flying Objects".

*

In the Firefly on the highway, Rawcus ambled along his pole and plunged his pink tongue into trance-striken Lennie's ear. "Giss a kiss, love!"

"Jesus Christ!" cried Lennie, brushing away the amorous beak. Lennie rubbed his eyes and slapped his cheeks to bring himself back to *the real world* as some people called it.

The commotion snapped Joe's thoughts back to the here and now too.

Rawcus shook his head in a parental way. "Wakey, wakey! Hands off snaky!"

Lennie rolled his eyes. Aunty D and her mates from the Rose & Thistle had taught Rawcus some colourful phrases, but it had Lennie beat as to how the bird timed his delivery. Lennie had just read in a science journal that sulpher-crested cockys possessed as many brain neurons as chimps and dolphins, but he'd never heard a fish or monkey talk.

"Spit it out then," Lennie said to Joe. "What did you want to reveal?"

"I saw the letter from the hospital. You left it stuck in the pages of that *Mice and Men* book you like so much."

"I knew there'd be trouble when you started getting gold stars at school," said Lennie, who for most of his life had never needed to worry about Joe picking up books that didn't have pictures in them. But that had changed in the last year.

The teacher of Joe's adult literacy class at community college had actually titled Joe's recent award "Highly Commended". But Joe had never landed a gold star at regular school so Lennie said they should translate his award into one that told a clearer, more colourful story which anyone could get their head around.

Soon after Joe won the award, however, Lennie had fallen into a secret place inside his own head that he called *The Cave*. In this place, he warred with confusing feelings about Joe becoming a star pupil. The feelings had long and tangled roots that went back to middle primary school where Joe could read little more than comic books, and even then he guessed what the words meant via the pictures.

This led Lennie to take on the role of Joe's "reader", starting behind the scoreboard at the sports oval after school where Lennie would bring his favourite adventure books. The reader-listener relationship continued into adulthood. But everything changed when Joe, wanting to relieve Lennie of this burden, had enrolled secretly to learn how to read and write.

On discovering this deception, Lennie had been pleased for Joe, but he had also started receiving an invisible visitor in *The Cave* from time-to-time. This visitor made Lennie's stomach feel like it was eating itself.

"When were you going to tell me?" said Joe

"Soon."

"Hep G can kill you, can't it? Cirrhosis, liver cancer?"

"Not necessarily."

"You'll have to give up the grog."

"Oh, yeah?" said Lennie. He didn't want to say so, because he didn't want to worry Joe, but ever since his diagnosis with this newly discovered and poorly understood strain of hepatitis, he felt like he had a ticking bomb inside him. The bloody GP had started all this by arranging a blood test after Lennie's foot was infected by a sprig of coral which he stood on while snorkelling on a reef. It wasn't the reef but prison where the liver virus stemmed from. Ignorance might not be bliss in all circumstances, Lennie believed, but in general, the idea had terrific merit. He wished he'd never had the blood test.

"Are there treatments?" said Joe.

"I'm talking to the specialist about it."

"You feeling alright now?"

"Strong as an ox."

Joe meant the question to be about Lennie's spirit, but it was clear Lennie was going to duck and weave his way through this round like the tricky boxer he was.

Joe shifted mental gears. "How do you reckon Pago got to our place?"

Lennie narrowed his eyes. "He didn't walk. Did you see his fancy footwear? Those Nike's were as white as Father Francesco's face the last time we saw him."

"He must have come in a truck or a car, or maybe a dirt bike."

"Dirt bike?" chuckled Lennie. "His bum would have swallowed that whole."

"Do you reckon came out alone?"

"Mm...too bad we didn't have time to check for footprints. Those coppers and Ken Milan have trampled the place now."

Joe slowed to let a wombat and its joey cross the road. "If he came out with some mates, surely they wouldn't have left him stuck on that cross."

Lennie rubbed his chin. "He does travel with that sort of crowd."

"I hate these sorts of mysteries," said Joe.

"Yeah, the old unsolved," said Lennie, reaching for the drink cooler. "Tell you what, I need an in-sighter."

As Lennie extracted a couple of beers, his phone trilled in its cradle on the dashboard. The name *Pauls* lit up the screen. He put the handset on open speaker so Joe could listen to the caller.

"Guys," said Pauline Gerrity. "I have bad news."

"Shoot," said Lennie.

"Bang! Bang!" cried Rawcus.

Lennie glared at the bird and waved an index finger.

Pauline said, "The Public Prosecutor has dropped the case against Toby Runyon."

"All charges?" Lennie growled.

"Yes. I think Runyon's father intervened again. He and his lawyer friends pulled some strings with the police."

"It's pretty handy having a judge for an old man," observed Lennie. "So where are Runyon's wife and daughter?"

"Holed up in my refuge. He is trying to have her sectioned again."

"The madness card, hey," grizzled Joe. "Shut up and take your medicine, or I'll put you in the nut farm and take your kid. Is that his game?"

"Yes, Joe."

Lennie massaged his brow. "OK. Joe and I are a bit tied up at the mo'. But let's whack Plan B into action for the time being. And then we'll get to work on Plan C."

"Thanks, Lennie." She sniffled. "Sorry...I think I'm getting a cold."

"She'll be right, Pauls," said Lennie.

After hanging up, Lennie arranged the fingertips of one hand on the crown of his shaven head and slid them gently down until his palm went flat. The sensation reminded him of warm raindrops falling. But it didn't relax him as much as usual and he couldn't stop thinking how tricky any Plan C would be to execute, not least because they didn't have one yet, and given all the plates he and Joe had spinning right now – including the one they had just dropped off a cliff and which might bounce back in unpredictable ways. And then there was the hopefully fading problem that involved his tomahawk and Mia and Karl from Gdansk. He touched the Jack in his pocket...

…an idea to deal with Mr Tobias B. Runyon fluttered into his skull like a Monarch butterfly breaking from a cocoon. Ha, thought Lennie, how can anyone live without a Jack in their pocket? There's no downside if it doesn't work, and only upside if it does. Maybe he'd sell them as merchandise one day. Free to friends and the financially challenged of course. Capitalism has merit but it needs boundaries.

"What's Plan C?" said Joe, who knew Plan B was simple and everlasting: Keep Your Chin Up.

"I think I've cracked it," said Lennie, snapping the cap on a beer and handing it to Joe. Lennie reached into his door's side-pocket and pulled out a dog-eared paperback: *Screen-writing for Dummies*.

"Remember that script I've been working on?" he said, sitting the paperback on his knee and cracking his own beer.

"*Slap and Tickle*?"

"Close. It's titled, *Just a Slap*. I need to get home and send an email."

Joe slipped an ABBA CD into the player and the voices of Frida and Agnetha burst from the speakers singing *Waterloo*.

Lennie and Joe joined in. Rawcus gripped his rod and coughed, pulling off a wonderful, crackling sound – but it had no effect on his companions. He shook his head as if he was travelling with idiots, flared his sulphur crest, and bobbed to the music.

PART 3 - COCOON

1 - THE CHEMIST

BLOOD ORANGE clouds tumbled across the Sydney city skyline, backlit by a rising sun.

Joe parked beside a row of century-old terrace houses. Rainbow lorikeets were going nuts in the branches of the street's paperbark trees, hanging upside down to chew pollen from the white bottlebrush flowers.

In the kitchen of their train-carriage-shaped terrace, Joe poured boiling water over black tea leaves inside a china pot and filled a small jug with cow's milk. Lennie toasted hand-cut slices of sourdough and smothered them with butter and salty black Vegemite. Rawcus, at the far end of the kitchen table, sipped fresh water from a shallow tin then turned his beak upon chili-dusted pumpkin seeds in a bowl.

Joe, after washing down his toast with tea, brushed his teeth. He put a sleepy Rawcus in his cage, which hung by a rope from a hook on the kitchen ceiling, and threw a blanket over the doorless cage. Joe trudged upstairs to bed.

Lennie stayed at the kitchen table and sent an email using the name, *Jill Parsons.*

He'd set up the email account through a Virtual Private Network that muddied the trails to his various online identities. VPN's could make it appear he was in any country he chose from Armenia to Zimbabwe. *Jill* was in Norway today.

Jill despatched her email to: *Mr Toby Runyon, Executive Chairman and Head of Entertainment, White Horse Film and TV Productions, Sydney, Australia.* Attached to the email was the outline of a screenplay for a film titled, *Just a Slap.*

Lennie washed down a pill and went to bed. The household snored through the day until nightfall.

*

"Next time I reach for a Halcion, cut my hand off," Lennie growled thick-tongued as he stepped naked into the kitchen and put the kettle on. He looked at the wall clock. At least it was a good time to wake up: 7.17pm.

Lennie checked the maths: 7's were odd numbers, as was a 1. And 7, plus 1, plus 7, equalled 15, which was also an odd number. Odd was always better than even.

Joe, stepping into the kitchen through the doorway from the back garden, carried a bunch of fresh-cut, sweet-smelling, white gardenias.

"We need to visit TC," Joe said, tucking the tall-stemmed flowers into the mouth of a vase on the kitchen table. "Tonight!"

"Ah, yes. The Chemist," Lennie grizzled. "Give me five."

He returned upstairs to his bedroom and dressed in a black T-shirt, black jeans, and black, elastic-sided boots. He closed his eyes and selected by touch alone a Jack from the timber box on his dresser. Lennie opened his eyes: the little-finger-shaped

Bloodwood charm had a pea-green painted fingernail. The other Jacks in the box had painted nails too, in shades covering a broad spectrum of the rainbow.

Lennie tucked the Jack into his fob pocket and wiped an eye gone watery at the memory of the woman who'd been more mother to him than great aunt. When Lennie was a kid, doctors had labelled Aunty D a *Polydactyl* and paraded her as a live exhibit at universities. Lennie had thought the label meant she was a type of dinosaur, but it turned out that she was catalogued and displayed because she was born with six fingers on her left hand. Her extra digit was the inspiration for the carvings that he now banked upon for a bit of luck in life.

*

In the dark of early evening, Joe cruised the Firefly past the front of The Chemist's apartment which was located on the first floor of a small, art-deco block in a side street of the suburb of Darlinghurst in inner Sydney.

Lennie, sitting in the front passenger seat, admired the triangular and rectangular geometry of the building's doors and windows in the short street upon whose footpaths towered old London plane trees with leaves that reminded him of outstretched human hands.

Rawcus dozed on his rod with his sleeping beanie over his head.

"I think we have a bird in the nest," said Joe, pointing up to The Chemist's balcony and a flickering light coming from inside which he assumed was a TV.

He double-parked at the back of the Darlo Bar hotel opposite the apartment building's entrance. Lennie climbed out to play sentry across the street from the building, and Joe drove away to look for the hen's tooth of an unoccupied car space in this part of the city.

Lennie leaned back against the pub's brick wall and studied TC's five-storey block. Funny, he thought, the people you meet on the job. Firefly Electrics had been recommended to TC by a mutual friend. TC had wanted to install some wall lights in his flat. After the installation, TC had mixed Pimm's and lemonade with fresh mint in a fancy glass jug. The trio soon discovered a shared interest in the growing of exotic plants under artificial lights.

Lennie knew from previous visits that there were two windows at the back of the flat through which TC could climb onto external drainpipes and monkey his way around the side of the building to the next street, or drop down to the back lane. And then there was TC's cave-like, street-front balcony for an escape using the knotted rope TC stored in a box by the French doors. In summary, he thought, it would be hard to catch the little bugger if he didn't want to be caught.

The building didn't have a lift; the main route to his flat was up an internal, polished-concrete stairwell, accessed through an unattended lobby. Lennie knew the passcode for the street-front security door – unless TC had changed it since their last visit a few weeks ago. He stepped across the street and tried the code; it didn't work.

He went back to the pub wall and waited for Joe. A variety of passing men and women offered him a variety of things: a hand-job, a palm-reading, a packet of happy pills, and a smack in the face. He politely declined all the offers, but the purveyor of the latter wouldn't take "no thanks" as an answer. So Lennie invited the offeror of the smack in the face to do his best. This led the man to withdraw the offer and invite Lennie into the Darlo Bar for a beer. Joe arrived as the hairy-backed stranger was stripping himself naked and asking Lennie how much he would charge him for a street-side, stand-up, full-body massage while the man clung to a tree trunk and mimicked a koala.

Joe stood beside Lennie, who informed him that TC had changed his passcode. "Guilty sign," Lennie concluded.

Joe was distracted by the disrobed man who hovered beside them, his facial expressions suggesting multiple personalities were darting about behind the man's eyes.

The hairy nudist appeared to select one of his characters. He put his hands on his hips and snarled at Joe: "What are you lookin' at, you ranga cunt? Never seen a birthday suit before?"

"We've already had this conversation, or one like it," intervened Lennie. "Is there someone we can call for you?"

"Are you stark raving mad?" said the stranger, who left his clothes and ran across the street, just missing the bumper bar of a taxi that rushed a red light.

"Want me to cover the back lane?" said Joe.

"TC's nimble, isn't he?" said Lennie. "You'd need to shoot him to bring him down if he makes a break around those drainpipes."

"I could ping him with a rock," said Joe, flush from his success at clocking Robbie from twenty paces in the bush. Joe scanned the road and footpath for an appropriate missile.

Lennie fingered his ear which was itchy where Toku Enoka's pliers had taken the old bite out of it in prison.

Joe said: "OK. Let's do it that way then."

"What way?"

"Play it by ear."

Figures were moving behind the glass panels of the chrome-framed front door of TC's block. Lennie and Joe quickly crossed the street and climbed a handful of steps to the outside landing. The door swung inwards and two happy-faced young women, holding each other's hands, appeared in the doorframe. One of the women held the door open so the boys could step in. Her pupils had consumed all but the faint outer ring of her green irises.

The dark holes reminded Lennie of a glassy sea on a moonless night where only the stars provided light. "Enjoy your evening in there," he said to the holes, wondering what it might be like to dive inside them, and what he might meet.

"Ta," she replied.

On the first floor, the entrance to flat 5B was blocked by a steel-barred, black-painted security gate, behind which stood an equally glossy black, flat panel door. About mid-way up the door was a fish-eye lens.

Lennie stroked the gate. "After what happened at the shed last night, these bars are giving me a creepy feeling."

"Do you reckon he'd booby trap his flat?" said Joe.

Lennie pondered possibilities and decided to move his eyes back to a safer distance. "He's full of tricks and likely frightened. He could spray sulphuric acid through that keyhole."

Joe stood tall so that if something nasty squirted out of the lock, it would land on his flannel shirt, not his face. He tried the gate's handle, but it was locked. He reached through the grill and swung a brass clapper into its receiver a few times. When the door didn't open, he decided he didn't have time to muck around getting the safety goggles from the van. He stared into the fisheye security lens and spoke loudly.

"Come on TC," said Joe, doing his best clown face to try and soften up the occupant. "Open Sesame."

The door stayed shut. Lennie took his phone from his pocket and dialled TC's number.

"Yes, Lennie," said a reedy voice.

"Open the door, TC," Lennie said firmly. "Hiding just gives you prolonged sweat. We've just been to *The End of the World*. You need to tell us what you know."

Behind the bars of the security gate, the panel door opened a smidgeon and a pretty little face peered from the gap. TC's ski-slope shaped nose would have slotted neatly into Joe's belly button if either man was in the mood for a hug.

Lennie tapped his left boot impatiently. "Does Joe have to tear your doors off? Or are you going to be polite?"

TC opened his main door and then unlocked the security gate using a medieval-looking key. The pale-faced young man surveyed the hallway like a meerkat bobbing from its hole and ushered Lennie and Joe inside. TC rebolted his doors.

Joe scanned TC. He was wearing a pair of navy-blue, tasselled boat shoes; cream chino trousers with a perfect centre crease; and a short-sleeved white polo shirt over biceps that made Joe think of peeled, soft-boiled eggs. TC had curl-free, mousy-coloured hair that he combed with a side-part that reminded Joe of schoolboy characters from 1950s TV shows.

"So, you've just been to *The End*," said TC. "Interesting trip?"

"Let's sit down and have a chat," said Lennie, who studied their reluctant host and reminded himself that although TC could pass for a teenager, boy or girl, the scientist identified as male and claimed to be twenty-seven years of age.

TC's front door had delivered them directly into his kitchen. In the middle of its chessboard-tiled floor sat a four-seater table with an apple-green Formica top standing upon chrome-plated legs. The table was surrounded by pristine white, contoured plywood chairs.

TC ran his eyes up and down his guests. His brow furrowed; his nose twisted. "Do you guys want to wash your faces and hands? And I'll make us a nice drink."

"Coffee, thanks," said Lennie, realising he hadn't washed properly since returning from the bush. Right now he felt as fresh as month-old lettuce. TC had obsessive-compulsive-disorder about cleanliness, Lennie remembered, and there was more to be gained tonight by catering to it than fighting it.

Joe looked at the dirt under his fingernails and a bloodstain on his forearm from Pago's gunk.

Lennie turned towards the hallway and the bathroom, and winked at Joe for him to follow. He swivelled back to TC, "We have some serious matters to discuss. So don't go throwing any of your sedative crap in there."

"Never to my friends," TC replied, sounding offended. "Towels are in the cupboard. Pop them in the laundry bin when you are finished."

To get to the bathroom, Lennie and Joe had to walk from the kitchen under a squared arch into the sitting room, and then down a corridor off which came two bedrooms whose doors faced each other. The bathroom adjoined the smaller of the sleeping rooms. All the walls in the flat were tall and painted spotless white, as were the ceilings. The polished timber floors were patterned in triangular shapes. The focal point of the sitting room was a cream-coloured sofa and two lounge chairs, all of which had thick armrests and lots of curves.

The furniture was edged with stuff that reminded Joe of thin, black liquorice. Joe had seen it all on Agatha Christie TV shows: TC had just copied the innards off Hercule Poirot's London flat. TC even had a palm in a pot. As he surveyed the flat, Joe realised that TC showed very little originality for a bloke with a big brain who could do amazing things with plants. But then, Joe figured, originality can be over-rated. Take the naked, hairy-backed guy doing the koala act in the street, for example.

Lennie, inside the black-and-white-tiled bathroom, looking into a stainless-steel framed mirror, saw that he needed a head-shave almost as much as he needed to know if TC knew anything about Pago Enoka. But the priority was understanding the circumstances of Pago's trip – because he had twin brothers who were as big as bulls and from whom a future visit was as likely as a cardiac arrest in the chest of a ten-a-day burger addict.

"Do you reckon he ever uses it?" said Joe, looking into TC's toilet bowl. The white dazzle hurt his eyes.

"He must shit into a bag," said Lennie, "and dispose of it off-site."

"Yeah. He looks like a dry pellet man. A rabbit."

When they re-joined TC at the kitchen table, which was now covered in a white cloth, the little man was nibbling a raw, purple carrot that he held over a large, white dinner plate. TC paused nibbling and pressed the plunger into a glass pot that was sitting on the table. The pot appeared to contain ground coffee beans and boiled water. Beside it sat two, spotless white mugs.

"You first," Lennie said to TC.

"I'm a tea drinker."

Lennie huffed impatiently. TC took a shot glass from a cupboard, half-filled it from the coffee pot, and sipped.

"Swallow," said Lennie. TC obeyed. Time passed.

"You OK?" Lennie asked TC.

"Sparkling, thanks." TC's head was bouncing like he had Parkinson's disease, but it often bounced, unassisted by any drugs or provoked by any physical ailments which Lennie and Joe were aware of. Joe called it *nerves*.

"*The End*," said Lennie pouring Joe a cup of coffee, then filling one for himself. "We were there most of last night, doing some tidying up. Any guesses about the subject matter?"

"Ah," said TC, throwing down the rest of his coffee like it was a shot of Tequila. "I was going to call you about that."

"When?" said Lennie.

"This very evening in fact."

"And what were you going to tell us?"

"Well, it was about Pago Enoka." TC gnawed his carrot with the lathe of his perfect little teeth. He kept the vegetable long but made it progressively thinner. The consumed carrot seemed to neutralise his shakes. He arranged its string core on his plate to display the twelve o'clock position precisely.

"We're all ears," said Lennie, whose hand travelled like clockwork to his plier-bitten sound-catcher.

Joe grinned at Lennie's movements: he couldn't tell if TC was a master manipulator or simply a weirdo. He concluded he was both.

"The man kidnapped me," squeaked TC. "He wanted to know where you kept the money from your stroke of luck on the wharf last year."

"And you said?"

"I thought it through."

"You thought it through – and took him to *The End*?" said Lennie.

"It worked, didn't it?"

Joe coughed into his mug, splashing the black fluid over his chest and hands. It spattered the white table cloth. Lennie put his mug carefully on the table.

"Don't worry, Joe," said TC. "It's a paper tablecloth."

"You sneaky snake," said Lennie. He had to give it to TC; he was tricky as. Because after rigging the spiked doorway, Lennie and Joe had thought it only fair to warn their botanical partner that such a contraption existed, just in case TC decided to visit out of the blue. And that was not a remote possibility, for they had discovered that TC was quite chaotic in his moods and habits.

It wasn't that Lennie and Joe were in love with TC. But he had skills they didn't have, and there was no point they could see in wasting on a steel spike a damned good brain with some special learning in it that they may wish to tap at a later date. So they told TC exactly where the spiked-cross was, and how the trigger worked.

"See that fancy toaster of yours over there," said Lennie.

"Yes," said TC, looking puzzled as to what relevance it had to the topic under discussion. "I have some bread and jam if you are hungry."

Lennie said: "I want you to run us through exactly what happened. Before, during, and after the main event with Pago. I can tell when you are lying. Your eyes twitch; did you know that? And if they twitch, I will take one of your hands, stick it inside that toaster, and cook it. Then we have your nose and dick as back up. Are we clear?"

Lennie scratched his nose instinctively, which annoyed him immensely because he'd read in a psychology book that such beak-scratching was a key indicator that a person was fibbing.

"Abundantly clear," TC replied without eye twitching.

TC explained that Pago had corned him in the laneway near the back door of TC's workplace at a medical pathology lab near Central Railway Station. Pago had been holding a pistol covered by a shirt draped over his arm.

"Pago was never going to take you guys on directly," TC added. "But he was watching your house. He saw me going in and out when we had our meetings, and he tracked me home, and to my work."

Pago had forced TC into the cabin of Pago's sports utility vehicle and grilled TC about where Lennie and Joe were hiding hundreds of thousands of dollars of used banknotes he believed they had scooped up off a city wharf when a bale of money, being smuggled out of the country by drug dealing agents for Islamic State terrorists, split open during a ship loading mishap months ago. The incident had been reported in the media, though Lennie and Joe were never publicly identified.

"Your secrets are safe with me," TC insisted. "But I had to tell him something. He was convinced you had that money, and that I knew where it was."

"OK," said Lennie. "I'm guessing you told him it was inside the shed."

"Oh, Lennie," said TC. "I have always admired your IQ."

"Get on with it," Lennie grunted, watching TC's left eyelid fluttering like a sparrow's wing.

TC overlapped his pencil-thin fingers and leaned on his elbows as if he was praying. "He made me drive his ute. He sat in the passenger seat watching hideous rap music videos on his phone, swigging Wild Turkey, waving his gun at me. I knew he was going to kill me for sure when he'd done with me. It was logical."

Joe said, "Hang on. *You* drove his ute on the freeway?"

"No need to be offensive," said TC. "It was an automatic. Plus you can adjust the steering wheel, bring the seat forward, and I was wearing my cowboy boots."

Joe glared at TC.

"Alright," said TC. "I had to sit on a folded picnic rug to see out the windscreen."

Joe raised his eyebrows.

"Alright," TC sighed. "And my briefcase."

Joe did a quick height calculation. "Fair enough."

Lennie grinned at his imagined sight of TC driving the giant ute. He would have been better off pushing the seat right back and standing behind the steering wheel as if he was the helmsman of a yacht.

TC said, "So I'm in the car driving. I had a couple of hours to figure out how to get him to open that side-door of the shed you told me about. I certainly didn't want him sending me in first, like some canary down a mine."

"So you drive up to the gate," said Lennie. "What next?"

"He jumps out. He's got a toolbox in the back tray of his ute. He gets a metal grinder out, a battery-powered thing. He's going to cut the gate chain. He's quite an arrogant man. He thinks he has me tamed by now. He's on foot, of course. I'm still behind the wheel."

"Then?" said Lennie.

"I fucked with his mind."

Joe chuckled and slopped his coffee.

Lennie rolled his eyes. "Method?"

"I called out the window to him: *There's a big wooden box in that shed. A treasure chest. The money's in there.* Pago's eyes lit up. So I said: *Be careful. There's CCTV above the roller door. Satellite-linked, back-to-base. So you don't want to get spotted. Make sure you go in through the wooden side-door. I think there's about half a million in there.* He just bolted. Grabbed a crowbar from the back of his truck, and rolled under the fencing wire with gold dust in his eyes."

"He's stupid," said Lennie. "But why would he be that stupid?"

"A bottle of Wild Turkey was rolling empty on the floor by the time we hit the dirt track," said TC. "He'd finished most of another by the time we reached the gate. And he'd been sniffing something entertaining up his nose from a packet that I just happened to have in my briefcase and gave him to try. Sadly I didn't have any sedatives at the time. Does that give you a hint about his state of mind?"

Joe squinted at TC: "You're a devious little man, aren't you?"

TC winked at Joe. "Thanks."

"And you?" said Lennie.

"I just sat in the truck listening to the silence. Pretty soon I heard this *thunk!* Then a bit of moaning."

"And?" said Lennie.

"It went quiet again. I have a weak stomach, as you know. I didn't want to have a look. So I sat in the ute listening to the radio – I love classic FM. I watched kangaroos nibble the grass and lyrebirds walking about. It was late afternoon and very relaxing, to be honest."

Lennie said, "Yeah, it is beautiful this time of year..."

Joe barked, "Get on with it." He could see Lennie's mind was drifting sideways along with TC's. It reminded Joe of being at sea on their yacht with Lennie saying "just let the wind blow us where it will" while Joe had to grab the tiller and make sure they didn't run aground on a reef or get rammed by a giant container vessel in a shipping lane.

"Yes, yes," said TC. "Let's stay on course...well, I must have waited for about half an hour. Pago didn't come back. I blew the horn a few times. No response. So I started the truck and motored back to the city, not all the way to my home, of course, considering trail of evidence issues and all that. I parked in a side street near Bankstown Railway Station opposite some public housing flats. I did the right thing and left the key in the ignition and the door unlocked.

"I thought it would make a nice, random gift for someone. They could re-birth it...and there were also some decent tools in the back that I knew wouldn't go to waste. I cleaned my fingerprints and DNA off the vehicle with some alcohol-based hand sanitiser I always carry. You can't be too careful, can you? Then I caught a train to the city and walked home."

"Very charitable of you," said Lennie. "And supporting public transport too. How long ago was all this?"

"Two days."

"And you were only going to tell us tonight?"

"I was in shock," said TC, who gently fiddled with the side-parting of his hair. "I assume he *is* dead."

"Unless his mum has stuck his head back on his shoulders and done some voodoo on him," said Lennie, beginning to wonder if TC was wearing a wig.

"And where exactly is the body?" said TC.

"Well, you might find it buried at *The End*," Lennie said, deciding that a strategic deception was in order.

"Oh."

"Yes," said Lennie. "And given that your name is on the property ownership title, an inheritance from your uncle as I recollect, I suggest it's best if we all stay mum on this subject, if you'll excuse the family puns."

"Yes. Mum it is," said TC.

Joe's phone started ringing inside his shorts pocket. He pulled the handset out. The name *Pauls* was on the screen. He stepped from the kitchen to the lounge room for privacy.

"What's up?" said Joe.

Pauline Gerrity said, "I just learned Toby Runyon has applied to the courts for permanent sole custody of their daughter. Jane Runyon is in a bad way."

"Where's Jane now?"

"She's in my refuge with her child. Her husband would love it if she was admitted to a psych hospital on suicide watch. So I'm staying very close to her."

"OK," said Joe. "I'll tell Lennie we need to hit the accelerator on Plan C."

"C?" said Pauline.

"Lennie has cooked up a cracker. Probably best if you do the three monkeys on this one and sit it out."

As Joe closed the call and re-entered the kitchen, TC walked to the sink and poured himself a glass of water. "What if the last of the Enokas come after me?"

"You'll have to get creative again," said Lennie.

Joe looked at TC, who started shaking. Joe said, "You've got our phone numbers, mate. Keep your head down and your door locked. Lennie and me will find out where they are."

"One other thing," said Lennie. "You said Pago stuck a gun in your ribs. Where it is?"

"Don't know."

TC's left eye twitched. Lennie nodded at the toaster, fighting the urge to scratch his ear.

"Well," said TC. "It popped out of his waistband as he rolled under the fence. It's inside my floor safe. Under my bed."

"Bullets?"

"Five."

"Keep it," said Lennie. Five was a good number. "And take this," he added, handing TC the green-fingernailed Jack from his pocket. "Touch it at least once a day."

TC looked aghast at the replica human digit.

Lennie said, "There's no harm in having a punt on the power of other dimensions. Call it secondary insurance – if you need to wrap it up in a little bow of logic."

TC curled his nostrils, pinched the Jack between the pads of a thumb and index finger, and held it at arm's length from his body. "Very generous of you, Lennie."

*

When Lennie and Joe climbed back into the Firefly and slammed the doors shut, Rawcus woke up cranky and shook his hood off.

"Whaat time d'ya call this?" the bird screeched. "Whaat time d'ya call this?"

In Rawcus's cry, Lennie heard the echo of his dressing-gown clad aunty scolding him as a teenager who'd broken curfew. Lennie dug in the glove box and opened a pill bottle of pumpkin seeds. He fed some to Rawcus. Lennie popped one in his own mouth and chewed.

Joe raised his eyebrows. "You that hungry?"

"Just wondering if they work on humans."

Their next-door-neighbour, Mrs Gianopoulos, a wildlife carer and naturopath had supplied the seeds which she dusted with powder from a herb called Valerian. She claimed the seeds calmed distressed animals.

Rawcus licked his beak clean and stepped gently from his rod onto Joe's shoulder. "Giss a kiss, love," he said.

Joe declined, but said, "Love you too, mate."

Lennie crunched. "Do you think he's really a bloke?" he asked through the pulp that was sticking to his teeth.

"TC?" said Joe, cruising the Firefly into the traffic. "I don't give a toss what sort of rig he's got in his pants."

"Me neither," said Lennie. "But if you're in a serious partnership with someone, it helps to know if they're hiding things."

"Sometimes we're hiding stuff from ourselves, mate, and we don't even know it."

"True," said Lennie, digging into a filing cabinet in his skull. "Freud called it *repression*."

"Freud?" said Joe. "Sounds like an Irishman ordering eggs for breakfast."

Lennie cleaned his side teeth with a fingernail. "These seeds aren't bad by the way. Taste-wise. But I'm feeling as wired as a dentist's chair. I need a proper tranquiliser." He reached into the drink cooler on the floor. He waved a can at Joe.

"I'm driving if you hadn't noticed," said Joe. "And we're surrounded by spies." He nodded at a police TV camera mounted on a pole at the intersection where he waited for the traffic lights to change.

Lennie popped the top on a can and sipped. "TC's parents must have been pretty weird, to throw something like him off their potter's wheel."

"Maybe that's why we get along with him," said Joe, accelerating on the green light.

"I reckon," said Lennie, who leaned back and closed his eyes, letting the rhythm of Joe's driving and the alcohol transport him. Inside his head, a picture wheel spun. The wheel slowed and an image came into focus: Lennie was six years old when his parents dumped him with his gran who still had most of her marbles at the time. He saw himself in short pants and a short-sleeved shirt, wearing squeaky leather sandals that he pretended were army boots because they made the same noise as his dad's as he marched past in an arm-swinging column on a street parade while Lennie held his gran's hand. That was the last he saw of his father, who vanished like a passing lightning storm.

Lennie whizzed the wheel forward, pausing in his mid-teens, the time when dementia started its long march into full-blown Alzheimer's in the old lady's brain. People had called her a "fruitcake". He had chuckled at the time: his gran didn't look like a cake, but the moles on her face did remind him of raisins. Lennie had enjoyed the freedom these circumstances provided, until his Aunty Doreen, who was really his gran's sister, turned up and provided guide-rails for his teen years that he only recognised as an adult. His aunt taught him how to read and write, and how to look at paintings in art galleries. How to "see beyond the surface of things" was the way she put it.

*

Joe glanced at close-eyed Lennie and sensed his friend was swimming through the past. Joe felt the urge to dive in beside him to make sure he didn't sink. That meant talking.

"When was it I moved into your gran's joint?" Joe said.

Lennie didn't open his eyes, but he spoke. "Winter. Gran thought you were her little brother come back from the war with the Japs in New Guinea. God, we laughed at that, hey?"

Joe remembered that the laughs didn't last very long. They stopped when the old lady kept asking him what it was like to be dead.

In the Firefly, Joe began sailing through his own memories which were ripped by lightning, by white flashes in a dark room. Inside the room, he saw a scrawny woman with pale skin, greasy hair, and sunken eyes, holding a smoking cigarette and slopping a glass of white wine. Near her, laying on her back on a bed, he saw a pre-teen girl wearing only a white singlet, and a pair of red sandals. A black wolf was standing at the foot of the bed holding a camera. Click! Flash! Joe saw himself peering through a window upon his mother, sister, and the male stranger.

Rawcus gently nipped Joe's ear, causing Joe to glance at Lennie who seemed to be slipping into a deeper trance.

"Ground Control to Major Tom," said Joe, reaching across and rubbing Lennie's bristly head. Lennie's eyes fluttered open.

Joe said, "We have the Cocoon of Man to focus on. Pauls rang earlier to say he's trying to snatch custody of the daughter. We need to go hard on Plan C."

2 - STRANGE PEACOCKS

THE MORNING SUN had drenched their flower-filled back garden with a "mellow yellow" light that would have delighted Impressionist painters such as Claude Monet, Lennie explained to Joe and Rawcus, who appeared to be listening politely to the art class into which they had been press-ganged.

Rawcus, standing on Joe's shoulder, began swinging his head in circles and moaning as if he'd eaten something unpleasant.

"Do go on," said Joe, diverting his rolling eyes from Lennie's gaze by picking up the garden hose and fiddling with the nozzle.

"Shut up!" screeched Rawcus.

"Bloody heathens," muttered Lennie, who read the mood of his uncultured audience and stepped inside the house to collect breakfast.

Lennie had learned about various schools of painting and descriptions of light from his aunt who was a handy practitioner as well as an appreciator. She did watercolours of flowers, plus excellent gloss work on the window frames and skirting boards in his gran's terrace house, which Lennie had inherited. These days, although technically dead, Aunty D drifted around the courtyard garden from time to time, at least from Lennie's point of view. But he couldn't see her this morning as he carried a laden tray from the kitchen through the back door, with an iPad tucked under his arm.

He placed the tray on a circular wooden table and unloaded a large plate stacked with Vegemite and mashed avocado on toast, together with a china teapot that was wearing a hand-knitted cosy, and two cups with saucers. There was also an ear of raw corn on the cob.

Joe dropped the hose and sat at the table. He poured cups of tea but was distracted by fizzing from a handful of electrical cables that were strung upon poles in the laneway behind their back fence. The spire of the Catholic Church up the lane was visible behind the poles.

"How old was Jesus when the Romans pinned him up?" Joe asked

"Thirty-three," said Lennie, sitting opposite Joe. "Same age as us."

"They didn't have electricity then."

"Not man-made. Not that I'm aware of."

"You reckon his dad could've fired a bolt at him. Would've saved the kid a lot of suffering."

"Yeah," said Lennie. "Some parents, hey?"

Joe stood, holding his saucer in one hand and his cup in the other with his little finger outstretched and inspected the narrow flower beds that lined the wooden paling fences.

"New kids have arrived," he called, admiring the green shoots that were born from a packet of native flower seed mix he'd been given to try by Mrs Giannopoulos. Mrs G had labelled her seeds, which she sold at weekend markets, *Pot Luck*.

Joe thought, forget that *Genetic Magnificence*, or whatever it was that TC called the GM stuff they'd been doing in the bush that sifted good plants from bad, the valuable from the worthless, in the hunt for the *Fountain of Youth*. As far as Joe was concerned, he'd love all the offspring he was about to get at random in his garden at home.

Lennie, who was chewing toast with one hand while flipping pages on his e-tablet, called to Joe, "Eureka! He's put his head in the trap now."

"Toby Runyon?" guessed Joe.

"Do dogs bite?" replied Lennie, who straightened his diaphragm to read aloud from an email authored by the boss of White Horse Film and TV Productions – and sent to Lennie's latest alter ego, *Jill Parsons*.

Joe scratched an itch through the white singlet that was stretched tightly over his weightlifter's chest, sensing wheels were turning that he could not stop, and that he was not inclined to want to stop.

Lennie read: *Dear Jill. Thank you for sending me the outline for your screenplay,* Just a Slap. *I think your drama about domestic violence is witty, funny, and it kept me turning the pages.*

"That's great," said Joe. "Maybe he gets it."

"Hang on."

But I'm sorry Jill. I am going to reject your script. The truth is, at the end of the day, it lacked authenticity. The way you described the violence in key scenes, particularly the wife turning the tables on her husband at the end, just didn't sound like the real deal to me. Good luck pitching it elsewhere. Best wishes, Toby.

Joe dug a thumb into his scalp behind an ear to grind some muscle fibre that was tangling in its usual spot. "He does have special subject knowledge."

Joe recalled the day he and Lennie had first seen Runyon's wife at Pauline's refuge where they had been repairing an air-conditioner. Looking out a window from Pauline's office, they had observed a seal-eyed woman sitting alone on a garden bench smoking. Pauline explained that the woman had received "a message" from her husband that had bruised her kidneys and put blood in her urine, at least that is what Jane Runyon said. Her husband told inquirers that his mentally unstable wife's "drinking problem" had flared again and she had fallen – again. This time Jane had broken a tooth and split a lip on the stairs. The police agreed with poor Mr Runyon's mental health assessment of his wife. Runyon, the son of a Federal Court Judge, was worried that his wife's erratic behaviour was psychologically damaging their twelve-year-old daughter.

In their garden, Lennie tapped his tablet screen. He was a wizard with Photoshop and had created an album of artificial characters, made by blending the heads and bodies of apparently real people whom he found on the internet. "How about this one?" he asked Joe.

"Oh, yeah," said Joe. "Skin like golden treacle. Smile to melt hearts."

The photo was of a girl – Lennie's mind's eye placed her in her early twenties – stepping from the surf, all wet and dripping. He dreamed, and drafted on his tablet an introductory note:

Dear Mr Runyon, my name is Audny Olsen. I am newly arrived in Australia from Norway. I have worked in drama production, including on Game of Thrones *in Ireland. I am looking for a role in film and TV production in Sydney, any level to start. I am sorry for this short notice, but you come so highly recommended. I am meeting a girlfriend at the Shakespeare Hotel about 6pm this evening, which is near your office I see on your website. I am happy to come to you, but if you would like to meet me for a drink that would be very nice. Sorry if I am being very forward. Yours, Audny*

PS: I have attached my photo, so you can recognise me.

"Mate," said Lennie, whose eyes remained focused on his screen. "Can you get me one of the spare phones...please?"

Joe stepped into the garden shed where he admired an old electric chair. Recently, he and Lennie had wired new chairs into a chain of dentists' surgeries. They had kept one of the unwanted recliners and put it in the shed where they powered it up. Joe entertained ideas about making it into a seat for watching TV or sleeping in the house. But for the time being, it had simply turned the shed into a multi-purpose guest room. Joe extracted a phone from a cupboard drawer and put a fresh battery and SIM card in.

In the garden, he handed it to Lennie, who typed the note from Audny as a text message into the phone and loaded her photo to accompany it. He sourced the mobile number for Toby Runyon from the emailed reply to *Jill Parsons* about her rejected screenplay, and hit Send.

"OK," said Lennie. "Want a bet he'll bite?"

"If he doesn't, *you* clean the shit out of Rawcus's cage."

Rawcus was standing on the courtyard paving beside his cage, stripping his corn cob. At the mention of the word "shit", Rawcus had turned his head sharply to face Lennie and Joe.

While they appreciated it took Rawcus a lot of effort to perfume his cage with his essence, there was a point at which hygiene needed to override three-dimensional art. And that point was nigh. Airing it in the garden could only achieve so much.

"You're on," said Lennie.

"What are you thinking?" said Joe. "We christen the electric chair with Toby and have a chat with him?"

"That's Plan D, I reckon."

"So run through Plan C for me."

Lennie and Joe workshopped the plan, consuming the rest of the tea and toast. Rawcus chewed his cob to the core...

Lennie placed his empty cup in its saucer. "I know we've got plenty of rope and gaffer tape, but do we have any of that yellow spray paint left?"

"He hasn't replied yet," said Joe.

There was a ping from Audny's phone. Lennie read his tablet screen and grinned like the Cheshire Cat.

"Shit," Joe grumbled.

Rawcus swung a fierce gaze at Joe, hopped into his cage, and started bobbing like a cage fighter who was raring to go.

*

In the late afternoon as the sunlight faded, Joe led Lennie into the front bar of the Shakespeare Hotel in Surry Hills in inner Sydney, close to Toby Runyon's office.

To Joe, the air smelled like the old underpants that he had dipped in bleach and water and used to clean the bottom of Rawcus's cage. Rawcus was at home sulking. Joe was sporting a bandaid on a bitten knuckle.

The Shakespeare was a magnet for chattering young men, most wearing beards, and spaghetti-thin girls who rarely looked up from tapping their phone screens using their brightly-coloured talons. Lennie and Joe were both dressed in black and didn't look too out of place.

Lennie purchased tall glasses of beer and they found an empty table and chairs beside a wall of nicotine-coloured tiles. He was carrying a bulging shoulder bag which he put on a third chair at their table.

"Remind me what Toby Runyon looks like," Joe said.

Lennie took his e-tablet from the shoulder bag and opened a photo of a chubby-faced man with a grey stubble beard and dark hair cut into a shape that reminded him of a German World War II army helmet. The man wore large, black-framed reading glasses.

While Joe studied the photo, Lennie pulled Audny's phone from his jeans pocket and typed a text message: *Hi Toby. I've just arrived at the Shakespeare. Will you be able to join me? x Audny.* He added a smiley emoticon with its tongue hanging out, thought better of it, and removed the tongue. He hit Send.

Runyon flashed back: *Just finishing a phone call. CU soon. T* "Quick," said Lennie.

They grabbed the shoulder bag and shot out of the pub, quickstepping down a shadowy side street to a slice of land wedged between double-storey, windowless, terrace house walls. The land was a patchwork of dirt and grass with a couple of scrawny gum trees to one side. The local council had whacked up a sign that said "Community Park". A concrete path ran diagonally through it. Night had fallen. There was no lamp post in the park, which relied on nearby street lights for illumination, so most of the lot was in shadow, especially the sides. Lennie and Joe stepped under a tree beside a wall.

From the shoulder bag, Joe extracted a black pillowcase and tucked the closed end into the back pocket of his jeans.

Two figures, lit by the distant street lamps, approached the diagonal walkway, coming from the direction of Runyon's warehouse office.

"Curveball," said Lennie. "He's bringing a mate. Wonder what they've got planned for little Audny."

"Never mind," said Joe, reaching for the shoulder bag. "I brought a spare sack."

"Hang on," said Lennie. "Here, give me a cuddle."

"What?"

"We're going to look like a right couple of shifty bastards if we just stand here in the shadows whistling *Waltzing Matilda*."

Joe chuckled. He held Lennie to his chest.

The walkers approached the hugging men "Get a room, faggots!" called one.

The chuckling walkers stopped to take a closer look; one swigged from a hip flask and passed it to his mate. Lennie and Joe released each other and faced the comedians, who had basketball-shaped guts, puffy faces, and piggy eyes. They wore matching, pale green polo shirts with the collars turned up, brown three-quarter length pants with button-up side pockets, and were shod in white trainer shoes with low-ankled white socks.

"You off to a fashion show, lads?" said Lennie, staying in shadow. "Doing a bit of catwalk stuff, eh?"

The walkers' mouths opened but they uttered not a sound.

"Meow!" said Lennie, scratching the air with the fingers of one hand that reached out of the gloom. "Whoof!" barked Joe.

The walkers took off at a quick step leaving little farting noises as they went.

"Look," said Joe, pointing. On the footpath in the direction the walkers had come from, a lone figure in a dark business suit loped purposefully, holding a phone to one ear.

Lennie and Joe backed into the shadows. From the bag, Joe handed Lennie a black baseball cap which he pulled onto his head and tugged low over his brow. Joe donned a balaclava that he rolled down over his entire face; there were good-sized eye holes and a decent slit for breathing through his mouth. But Joe mainly liked a full balaclava because his red hair could be unhelpfully distinctive on these sorts of jobs. They separated like a splitting amoeba, Lennie sliding left along the wall, Joe sliding right.

Runyon was so focused on his phone conversation that he didn't notice Lennie and Joe as they stepped onto the path, putting Runyon smack bang between them, Lennie at his front, Joe at his back. Lennie thrust a shoulder into Runyon's side as they crossed.

"Watch out, fuckwit!" yelled big-bodied Runyon, who dropped his phone from the impact. He squatted, picked up his handset, and popped it inside his jacket pocket. As he straightened, he plunged his head into Joe's waiting pillowcase.

"What the fuck!" Runyon growled, trying to spin away.

Grasping one of Runyon's hands, Lennie twisted so that Runyon's arm turned up behind his back. Joe grabbed yelping Runyon's necktie and jammed the knot against his Adam's apple.

Joe dragged the gurgling man by the leash of his tie with Lennie at the man's back using the buckled arm like a steering rudder. They shuffled into the shadows beside the wall.

Lennie let go of Runyon's arm and took the gaffer tape from the shoulder bag. He passed the tape to Joe and turned away to watch the path for possible witnesses.

Joe tugged the pillowslip firmly down over Runyon's head and strapped the tape several times around the sack, covering the spot where he figured Runyon's mouth would be, but leaving his nose uncovered. After loosening Runyon's tie, he taped the pillowslip lightly around his throat to make sure the hood didn't slip off. Then he strapped the moviemaker's wrists together in front of his belly. Joe tripped Runyon onto the ground and taped his ankles together. Runyon bucked, so Joe taped his legs together at the knees which subdued him quite a lot.

Lennie knelt beside Runyon and listened to his breathing.

"He'll live," he whispered to Joe.

Joe set to work with another roll of tape, starting at Runyon's shoes and ankles. It took half a dozen rolls and many minutes to encase Runyon in black tape, moving up from his feet and legs to his torso and arms. Joe did a few more turns around Runyon's face, but kept the collar area loose and his nose free. Apart from those spots, Runyon was completely encased in shiny black tape. Joe flashed a thumbs-up at Lennie.

Joe rolled the balaclava up off his face, but kept it on as a beanie to hide his hair. Lennie kept his cap low on his brow and hand-signalled to Joe to pick up his shoulder bag and follow him to a spot out of hearing distance of Runyon.

Lennie whispered: "You got the sunnies?"

Joe reached into the bag. "You sure about this? It's night time. We are going to look seriously dodgy."

"So we need to look so seriously dodgy people will think we are a joke."

Joe chuckled. Just about everyone they met thought he and Lennie were a joke.

Joe pulled two pairs of owl-eye sunglasses from the bag and handed a pair to Lennie. They put them on.

"Aw, bit hard to see at night, isn't it?" said Lennie, who nodded at the bag. "Let's have a shot of that parting gift from Mia to brighten the light."

Joe reached into the bag for the hip flask of ether that she had given Lennie in the forest. They took a hefty swig each.

Lennie wiped his lips. "When the going gets weird, the weird turn pro."

"Let's hope so," said Joe, who recognised the quote Lennie had plucked from a book he'd read to Joe. It was written by some dead American named Hunter S. Thompson. Joe liked a few drugs, but Hunter's characters had gone way overboard. Lennie said the guy was the father of Bozo Journalism, or maybe it was Gonzo. But Joe wasn't in the mood for a Lennie lesson right now.

They emptied the flask and Joe put it back in the shoulder bag. He extracted two pairs of thin black leather gloves, giving the small pair to Lennie. Joe slung the bag over his shoulder. Donning the gloves, they returned to Runyon's side.

Joe, facing the same direction as Runyon's head, bent down and put his right arm around Runyon's chest. Lennie, standing on the other side of their captive, draped his left arm around Runyon's knees and used the fingers of his spare hand to signal: one, two...on three, they lifted Runyon off the ground.

Runyon began sliding from Joe's grip; he was heavier and slipperier than Joe expected. The shiny tape didn't help. Joe took a fresh bite and squeezed harder on his load. A few murmurs and the sound of breaking wind uttered from inside the cocoon as they marched out of the park and up the street.

"How's the light?" Lennie whispered to Joe, wanting to limit the chances of Runyon identifying him or Joe by voice recognition down the track.

"Good," said Joe, who noticed a lot of objects they passed were wearing neon halos. Timber lampposts that were usually grey, were outlined in red. What was in that Polish spirit?

Minutes later they turned into main Crown Street, joining a footpath bustling with strange peacocks.

The strutting creatures were mostly young adults wearing expensive clothes and smug expressions. Many of the males wore slim-fitting suits or body-hugging shirts and held their beaks at jaunty angles, routinely checking their reflections in shop-front windows to groom the feathers on their heads, or stroke their eyebrows if they had few or no crown feathers to play with. Odd mobs of grey-quilled males and dye-plumaged females, many with dazzling white teeth, applied themselves earnestly to impersonating the younger peacocks.

Lennie's and Joe's hunt for the right tree for Toby Runyon took them past packed, moodily lit bars and restaurants. The males and females occupying the window seats in the busiest places reminded Lennie and Joe, not of the birds of paradise in the street, but of gold-toothed rats sitting on blocks of cheese that they were yet to eat. It appeared to the young electricians that these rats may never eat the cheese because they would lose their prime positions and the envious looks of the other rats.

The shadow-men came to a towering plane tree growing out of the footpath beside a crosswalk.

"Perfect," Lennie whispered to Joe. "Let's do it here."

Lennie calculated there was plenty of foot traffic to provide an audience, as well as good viewing to be had from passing vehicles. The tree itself had, extending from its main trunk, a sturdy branch that ran parallel to the footpath, at about twice Joe's height, and did not protrude into the road.

They carried Runyon to a spot not so close to the crosswalk that they would stop traffic, and dropped him on the footpath. They adjusted their caps, gloves, and sunnies, which had been thrown slightly out of kilter by the walk.

Joe placed the shoulder bag on the pavement and removed from it two lengths of thick black rope. He soon had the ropes secured to the bough above, with the ends coiled on the footpath. As Joe tugged the rigging to check the strength of his ties, Lennie walked away and turned down a lane, heading to the parked Firefly.

From the van, he collected three lengths of bamboo cane, each as long as his leg and as thick as his little finger. Moments later, he was back at Joe's side, leaning the canes against the tree trunk.

Joe was tying one of the ropes to the foot-end of the wrapped man; he felt a tap on his shoulder and looked up: Lennie was pecking the air with an index finger, pointing at two figures approaching them at a range of about fifty paces.

The figures wore the light blue, short-sleeved shirts and navy trousers of the New South Wales Police Force; their utility belts bristled with more artillery than Robbie and Arty had carried.

Lennie, staying mute, tapped his finger on his own chest, nominating himself to tackle the officers. Then he pointed at

Runyon, signalling for Joe to keep working on the installation. The officers hastened as they zeroed in on the sight of the ropes and the black bundle on the footpath. Lennie cut them off about a car's length short of their target.

"Good evening officers," he said brightly, wondering if he should remove his sunnies. He'd listened to a podcast by a psychologist who said that showing an open face gives you a better chance of persuading someone that you are telling the truth – nose scratching and eye twitching giveaways aside. Lennie decided to keep the sunnies on and play this by ear, inadvertently stroking his mutilated lobe.

"What's happening here?" said the male officer, moving his plump head sideways to look around Lennie's shoulder.

Lennie figured his inquisitor was aged in his late twenties and liked eating given he was shaped like a potato and carrying a half-eaten hamburger in its wrapper. His taller, freckle-faced female partner had a blonde ponytail and resembled a greyhound.

"We're installing an artwork for the Sydney City Council," said Lennie. "It's part of a project called *Metamorphosis Week* that's happening all around the world."

"Is that right?" said the male officer, who bit his burger and changed his lean to the other side of Lennie so he could get a better line on the figure working on the ropes.

"Yes," said Lennie.

The copper wiped his lips with his fingers. "Does your artwork have a name?"

"*Cocoon of Man.*"

"Looks like it's moving," said the female officer.

Lennie turned to follow the line of her gaze. Sure enough, Runyon was managing the very slightest of wiggles on the footpath. Lennie heard low grunting coming from Runyon's pillowslip. A phone started ringing inside the cocoon.

"Shit," Lennie muttered. He'd forgotten that Runyon had popped his phone inside his jacket pocket at the park.

"Is there are a problem?" said the female officer.

Lennie ruminated for a few seconds. He said, "There are some high-tech mechanics built into the sculpture. It gives it a powerful sense of realism, don't you think?'

"It certainly does," she replied.

The male officer said: "So you are going to hang...what did you call it...*Cuckoo Man*...from that tree?"

"Those are our instructions from the council and the artist."

"And who is the artist?" asked the female officer.

"Oh," said Lennie, rubbing his chin. Thoughts bounced around his skull like coloured lights off a twirling disco ball. He snatched a green ray.

"The artist's name is FoFo," said Lennie, channelling the voodoo craft of Pago Enoka's mum.

"Is he local?" said the female officer.

"Yes and no," said Lennie, wondering why she would guess the fully-covered FoFo was a man and not a woman. While FoFo was large, Lennie figured the officer should visit a suburban shopping centre or two to see how some of the human species were evolving into a universal form.

The female officer furrowed her pointy brow. "Does he always wear that mask pulled over his face?"

"FoFo is shy," explained Lennie, who looked back at Joe, who now had the balaclava unfurled to below his chin, with his eyes still covered by the sunglasses.

Joe had hauled the bottom half of Runyon off the footpath by the ankles and tied that rope in place. He was now securing the second rope around Runyon's chest. But the sight that made Lennie's eyes pop wide open was the crowd of people who had gathered to watch Joe work. There were at least a dozen men and women in a semi-circle. As he watched, the mob was joined by others, including a schoolgirl in uniform with a black poodle on a lead that sniffed the pavement-level head of the cocoon and shaped as if it was going wee on it. The cocoon wiggled and the dog barked suspiciously. Runyon's phone rang. The mob began taking selfies against the backdrop of the half-hoisted cocoon, while Joe tugged the ropes, lifting Runyon's upper half with the skill of a sailor at his rigging.

"Fascinating," said the male officer. "He certainly draws a crowd."

"I really must get back and help FoFo with the installation," said Lennie. "Nice meeting you."

"Likewise," said the female officer.

"Wait on," said the male officer, popping his burger wrapper into a street bin. "Do you have a permit?"

Lennie had hoped it wouldn't come to this. He reached into his jacket pocket and unfolded a sheet of A4 paper onto which he had printed a letter with the City of Sydney logo that he'd cut and pasted off the city's official website. The letter was headed *Metamorphosis Week* and the text welcomed international artists to Sydney "to express their ideas about social change in imaginative ways across the city". Lennie had forged the signature of the Mayor, Helen Caraway, at the bottom of the letter.

"Here you go," Lennie said, handing the letter to the officer.

The officer studied the paper using his torch. Lennie was glad he and Joe were wearing their running shoes. Burger boy wasn't a worry, but greyhound girl displayed disturbing athletic potential. The officer waved the sheet as if he'd made a discovery.

"*Installation 17: Cocoon of Man.* What a great idea," the officer said. "Good luck with it all." He folded the letter neatly and handed it to Lennie.

"Do you mind?" the officer said, offering his phone to Lennie in order that he and the greyhound might be photographed with FoFo and the cocoon. Lennie adjusted his sunnies, tugged his cap lower, and obliged. The officers turned and walked back the way they had come.

The flashes of other selfie-snappers blazed as Lennie stood beside Joe, who was tying off the ropes around the tree trunk, fixing the cocoon horizontally at about adult chest-height. Lennie reached into the shoulder bag and found the can of yellow spray paint. He rattled the atomising pellet.

"Oh, yeah!" shouted a couple of unsteady young men, who started clapping along with Lennie's clacking pellet, finding a counter rhythm. One began dancing a jig. A barefoot girl in a flowing white dress joined the dance, specialising in twirls that almost spilled her off the footpath onto the road and into the moving cars. FoFo stepped over and guided her back to the pavement.

Lennie stopped shaking the can and stepped in towards the cocoon. He sprayed *Hit me!* on each side of it.

"Yo!" yelled the jazz clappers.

Laughter and cheering burst from the crowd. Joe was demonstrating to the bystanders how to whip the cocoon with the bamboo canes. He offered the canes to the crowd, but everyone appeared frightened to approach his hulking dark figure.

The schoolgirl with the dog was bravest and eventually took a cane. Joe held her dog's lead. The girl tapped the cane against the cocoon, which bucked slightly, unleashing roars of delight from the mob. The phone rang. Two young women in cocktail dresses, high-heeled shoes, and hoop earrings took the other two canes and circled the cocoon looking for the right spot to land a blow.

The crowd clapped, stamped, and chanted: "Hit me! Hit Me! Hit me!"

So the women did, and the beast bucked and the crowd bellowed for more.

With the growing mob in party swing, Joe collected his shoulder bag and he and Lennie slipped away, quickstepping the back streets to the Firefly.

As Joe started the van, Lennie reached into the drink cooler, opened a couple of beers, and handed one to Joe, who downed the can in one hit.

He handed the empty container to Lennie and winked. "You know I never drink *and* drive." Joe took his balaclava off, fluffed his hair, and moved off.

Lennie had a swig. "Let's swing past and get an update on the public reaction."

Joe drifted along Crown Street at a sedate pace so as not to arouse attention, but also so they could cop a decent view. The crowd was swarming around the cocoon like ants over a dropped lolly.

As Joe scanned the mob, the number *41* flashed in his brain: 41 people. He had a knack for counting without thinking, like being able to glance into a cutlery drawer and know instantly how many knives and forks were in there.

The mob was sharing the canes, taking turns to smack the cocoon which was wiggling, and rocking backward and forward like a swing with a ghost rider.

"Where there's movement, there's life," said Lennie, who told himself that if Runyon's black heart was going to give out, it would most likely have done so before they put him in the tree.

"Enough?" said Joe.

"Getting close, I guess," said Lennie. "But when you put a halo on your head by making free TV adverts for White Ribbon Day to stop violence against women, then slip home to bash your wife below the neckline, and call your Judge dad to get you off the hook, you should get some of your own medicine."

"Yeah. He's gettin' a good dose."

"I don't reckon it'll cure him. But it'll give him food for thought," Lennie added.

"Now you've done it," said Joe. "I'd kill for a chicken kebab."

"Just had the same idea. That ESP thing of ours must be working again. I thought it might be going on the blink. One last job though."

Lennie used Audny's phone to dial 000.

A woman's voice said, "Police, fire or ambulance?"

Lennie straightened his diaphragm and said, "My dear. A large cocoon, at this very moment, is hanging from a tree on Crown Street in Surry Hills. There is a man inside waiting to be rebirthed. He'll need an ambulance and probably some psychological counselling. Cheerio." He hung up.

Lennie took the battery and SIM card out of Audny's phone. A few minutes later he re-inserted the parts and made a call from a different location, offering the police Crime Stoppers unit additional information about Runyon. Lennie couldn't be sure how his attempt at a female accent was going over but he gave it a solid crack. He hung up and disassembled the phone again. He worried that his credibility may have been affected by sounding like Rawcus trying to adopt a romantic tone. But there was naught he could do about that now.

They parked near a Lebanese restaurant which they entered and ordered chicken kebabs to eat at a table in a booth near the back of the premises where it was quiet and they could muster their thoughts.

In the booth, Lennie stroked the air with an index finger, writing in front of Joe's face in mirror-reverse.

"R-E-D," Joe deciphered. "I agree."

Lennie said, "Runyon was this close. This close..." He narrowed the gap between the pads of a thumb and index finger so there was the merest glimpse of light.

"Gotcha," said Joe. "He was very lucky to get a yellow."

*

The colour scheme was born adrift a glassy green sea aboard the *Flamingo Sky*.

Lennie had been leaning against the mainmast with the rigging clanking on the rise and fall of a gentle swell. Joe had been lying naked and face-up on a towel on the rear deck, admiring clouds that made him think of mashed-potato lambs.

Lennie had said, "You know, mate, people cook up – and keep – all sorts of nastiness in their heads. There's no stopping that, and nor should there be.

"But when you let it spill out through your hands and feet – or you shoot your mouth off in a vicious way – well, things change. Borders are crossed. People deliver hurt, and people get hurt."

"Uh, huh," Joe had said, fearing Lennie was drifting into space that only Lennie could understand.

"There should be consequences when you deliberately hurt someone who's done you no harm. Know what I mean?"

Joe's heart galloped; the clouds were turning from fluffy lambs into the darkly-furrowed face of a man with huge nostrils and hairy hands that were reaching from the heavens for Joe's body.

Joe jumped up. "Give me a sec," he said, kneeling by a gunwale. He cupped a hand and scooped it over the side, filling it with water which he splashed on his face trying to wash away the vision of his old headmaster, Mr Darian. Joe tucked the towel around his waist. "OK, I'm good."

"I'm talking here about failures in the system," Lennie continued, "where people literally get away with murder, and the like."

"Go on," said Joe, who glanced overhead, relieved that the lambs were returning.

"We need a rating system."

"Got something in mind?"

Lennie gazed at the shimmering horizon. "There are seven key colours in the rainbow, right? An odd number, which is important." He used his fingers to count them off: "Red, orange, yellow, green, blue, indigo, and violet."

"I think I'm getting it," said Joe. "Your gran's name was Violet."

Lennie flashed a thumbs-up. "I reckon that's it. Father Francesco would be a red, same as Darian. And everyone else is in between."

Lennie's faith in the odd-numbered, rainbow-coloured, rating system of human character was reinforced when he realised that no matter how small, or big, an odd number gets, if you shove a fulcrum under the middle number, the whole lot balances perfectly all the way to both ends of infinity. That was a scale of justice he could grasp.

Back at home the night after their day sailing, Lennie dug a book from the shelf in the lounge room and read a quote to Joe: "*I think there are certain crimes which the law cannot touch, and which, therefore, to some extent, justify private revenge.* Sherlock Holmes, The Adventure of Charles Augustus Milverton."

"Now," said Lennie. "Holmes was a pommy tosser, but he had a point. We're just sharpening it."

Lennie and Joe retired that evening after agreeing that if someone was an absolute prick who got away with murder or monstering a child or the like, such as Francesco and Darian, they got a red sticker. Orange and yellow were grades for lesser evils.

Green was neutral turf, but those people would come up for regular review.

Blues, indigos, and violets were indicators for top-shelf characters like Pauline Gerrity and, if they needed it, they received support, like cash, or being taken to the shops, or having their faulty washing machine and lights fixed for free.

Categorising people, of course, was a tricky task. In the end, it boiled down to "available evidence", and Lennie and Joe had different methods for obtaining evidence than did the cops or so-called Courts of Law administered by the State.

Under their system, there was no *Get Out of Jail Free* card like there was in the regular system that Sherlock Holmes also had a problem with, a system where a villain's lawyer could say stuff like "you didn't get that evidence the right way" and the case gets thrown out of court, even though it's clear the guy tossed petrol on his girlfriend and set her on fire – or in Runyon's case he used his judge father and his lawyer mates to cover up the fact he bashed his wife and molested his daughter, and set his wife up as an insane alcoholic.

Lennie and Joe dubbed their system *F for Ethics,* and it evolved over ensuing months. But it was not smooth sailing. For if Lennie rated someone by any colour at all, Joe would have a chance to argue the toss, and vice versa. Pauline was consulted on the latest project with Runyon because of her personal involvement in the matter via her women's refuge.

In the time they'd been operating *F for Ethics* they had never reached a stalemate, which was handy because they didn't have a clear resolution mechanism if they disagreed.

They'd thought about bringing Rawcus in and putting food dye on a couple of pumpkin seeds – one representing Lennie's selected colour and the other Joe's – and letting the bird choose the final colour. And they'd thought about a coin toss. But they concluded that both approaches were a tad casual, especially if red was involved. So they just argued for however long it took to reach an agreement.

*

As they stepped from the kebab shop, Joe said: "Are you seeing what I'm seeing?"

"If you're talking about a weird fog, then I think we are in this together," said Lennie.

Joe got behind the wheel and picked his way home through gloomy streets in mustard-coloured light.

Lennie said, "You'd want to lock your windows tonight."

PART 4 - WANTED: FOFO

1 - HELP!

THEY WOKE later than usual. Lennie reckoned they over-slept because the mustard mist had thickened overnight and smudged the arrival of dawn's light to which their optic nerves were tuned and their body clocks set. Joe reckoned they'd slept in.

They made tea and toast and turned on the TV in the lounge room looking for clues to what was happening to the world.

It was a climate event, El Nino-related, the weather experts explained. A massive cloud of dust had been stirred by winds over drought-affected inland plains. The cloud had travelled east on the prevailing winds. After blowing over the Blue Mountains it had dropped in the cooler air upon the coastal lowlands and blanketed the entire metropolis of Greater Sydney. The winds had now died. The dust may take days to disperse.

"Can you read that?" said Lennie, who was following a string of words crawling along the bottom of the TV screen.

"Enough of it," said Joe, going wide-eyed.

Lennie used the TV remote to turn up the volume.

A female reporter was standing on the steps of a police station: *Armed police officers from the tactical response squad have this morning captured the fugitive killer, Kenneth Michael Milan, on an isolated property in the southern Blue Mountains west of Sydney. Milan has been on the run for almost a year, evading police across rural communities in several States. He is believed to have murdered at least four people. Milan is currently being questioned in the police station behind me. Police will not confirm reports that Milan's latest victims were a young couple, possibly bringing his tally of murders to six...*

Lennie thumped the low table, causing the cups and saucers on it to jump and spill.

"We got Mia and Karl to the main road, mate. They should have been long gone," said Joe.

"What if they got lost again?"

Lennie had a second thought: what if Ken Milan spills to the cops about Pago Enoka and the spiked cross?

Joe righted the teacups. "I know what you are thinking. The coppers could go out there with those body-hunting dogs."

"Cadaver dogs...yeah."

"They'd need to be good abseilers."

Lennie squeezed his skull as if he might milk insight from it. He concluded that his bristly brain-case needed a shave. He could grow hair, plenty of it. But at Sunday school camps, Father Francesco had liked to run his hands through his locks and grip his curls to pull Lennie's mouth in when he wanted to use it. Lennie's phone rang.

It was an emergency call-out for Firefly Electrics from the manager of a nursing home. The dust had stuffed up their air-conditioning units and sparked an electrical fault that sent the fire alarms into mania.

"We've got an urgent job, mate," he said to Joe. "We better get cracking."

Joe said, "You've got her number. Call it."

Lennie dialled and put his phone on open speaker. They got a voice message in a foreign language.

"Hi, Mia and Karl. Lennie and Joe here. Hope all's well. Please call to let us know you're OK."

*

By the end of the working day after fixing the air condition-ers, they were knackered and thirsty and walked to the Rose & Thistle a few blocks from home for steaks and beers. It was about 10pm when they left the bar and the yellow dust was still hanging around.

"Funny," said Joe, as they walked in the gloom under the brick arch of an old railway bridge. "We could be in one of those movies about Jack the Ripper. I know we've had a few grogs, but I can almost hear the clip-clop of horses' hooves and squeak of carriage wheels."

Lennie tapped Joe's arm. They stopped in silence under the arch.

A train rattled and screeched along the tracks above. The rumble faded. They listened: nothing but the whine of mos-quitoes wanting their blood. Lennie shrugged and smiled. The fog was making him paranoid. They walked.

Joe lifted a hand in a stop sign. They pulled up, still under the bridge. The *ker-slap, ker-slap* of rubber thongs striking the soles of feet echoed. They turned to face their follower...

"Good evening," boomed a huge figure emerging from the murk. John Enoka grinned with a froglike mouth, revealing a missing incisor.

Like his dead brothers – Jona, Toku, and Pago – the main difference between John's body and a bull's was that John walked on hind legs. The earth seemed to shudder with each of his flip-flopping steps, and his hide wobbled like jelly dessert. He wore grey track pants and a loose grey T-shirt. Despite the mist, there was no mistaking the pistol John held in his hand.

Moving their heads like synchronised swimmers, Lennie and Joe examined the hand which was holding his gun: John's fat index finger was squeezed inside the trigger-guard. All it needed was for him to sneeze from the dust; jump at the surprise emergence of a passer-by; or flinch at a mosquito biting his ear.

"Hullo, boyce," said a squeaky voice behind their backs. They turned to face Chris Enoka.

Lennie, who had first encountered the twins in a prison common room when they visited their elder brothers, figured that maybe a fun-loving sibling had whacked Chris's voice box with a fist or a stick when he was younger, or made him drink bleach, to give him that unmistakable squeak. The Enokas were those sorts of funsters.

Blocking an exit under the railway arch, Chris carried a headless axe handle and slapped it against an open palm with a slow beat.

"So nice of you guys to visit our tunnel," said Lennie. "I guess you left the chocolates and flowers in the car."

"Listen, wiseguy," said John, lifting his arm to point his barrel at Lennie's face. "You have something that belongs to friends of ours and they want it back."

"What might that be?"

"The cash you cunts stole off that wharf."

"That's a rumour."

"Our bro's say *you* got it. Most of it."

Lennie and Joe huffed like marathon runners who thought they'd crossed the finish line, only to be told there was another lap to go. It was true they'd been fishing on a city wharf a while ago, when a bale of waste paper dropped from a crane during a cargo loading accident. The bale split open and showered the dockside with cash that was being smuggled overseas, news reports said later. Lennie and Joe had been wearing hoodies and the wharf's CCTV cameras couldn't identify them. The media reported that the broken bale – one of thirty loaded, or waiting to be loaded on a ship – was linked to drug dealing by the connections of Islamic State terrorists and destined for shipment to surviving IS offshoots in North Africa, South-East Asia and the Middle East.

There was about $30 million in all, around $1 million in each bale. Half the cash in the broken bale was recovered on the wharf on the day. Lennie and Joe escaped with $200,000-odd. But the investigating coppers put it to the media that the unidentified thieves made off with $500,000-plus. So Lennie and Joe figured the cops took $300,000 for themselves and tried to stiff them with swiping all the missing cash.

"Well your bro's were mistaken," said Lennie.

Chris, apparently unhappy at the suggestion his dead bro's were boneheads, swung his axe handle at Lennie's left knee. Lennie twisted, causing the handle to strike the outside of his joint and miss the kneecap at which it was aimed. He fell to the footpath, reaching for the impact point to dampen the fire inside his bones.

Joe moved to shield Lennie. Chris took a backswing for a second strike. *Ka-thack!* The men were showered with crumbs of brick. John's bullet had raked the roof of the tunnel.

"The next one's for your nuts, Lennie," promised John, grinning, aiming at the nominated target area.

As Lennie lay on his side and clutched his knee, he realised he would need to take more punishment. Not just because the last of the Enoka brothers were torchbearers for sadism. No, he would need to take more punishment if he was going to persuade the Enokas of the story he was cooking up. For if he volunteered the existence and location of the missing wharf money too easily, the Enokas would think it was bull-shit, even if it wasn't. It was tricky business, managing the brains of bulls.

Lennie glanced at Joe. Lennie was already down, so he reasoned that he might as well suck up the rest of what was coming. But he needed to do it in a way that would not provoke Joe to heroics. For what was the point of Joe being hurt too? Surely it was better, practical to be precise, that one of them at least should stay in fully fit, working condition so if the chance to escape from this situation arose, they could grasp it with the maximum possibility of success. But, thought Lennie, how do I hook that logic into Joe's head?

Lennie reached into his jeans pocket and touched his Jack.

Whoomp! John had driven the toes of his right foot into Lennie's torso, striking the soft spot between his ribs and the hip joint where a kidney resided. Lennie groaned. Joe looked into his friend's eyes. Lennie winked at Joe, who bit his lip and shook his head; he got the message alright, but he didn't like it.

"Listen," said Joe. "I don't know what sort of weird trip you guys are on, to think we have the cash from that wharf. But if you need a bit of dosh to buy ya mum something nice for her birthday, we can make a contribution. Can't we Lennie?"

"Like fuck we can!" yelled Lennie, dragging himself across the footpath. He propped with his back against the arch wall. He braced for the reaction to his latest act of defiance. Just don't shoot me, he thought, that'll throw Joe into a complete frenzy. And the outcome of that, with an Enoka holding a gun, would be as predictable as legally blind drunks throwing punches in a bar.

Chris advanced with his axe handle – and smashed Lennie's hand which was protecting his knee. Lennie grunted: "Cheers."

John wobbled to Lennie's side, leaned, careful not to tip over, and slapped the side of Lennie's face with his pistol. As his hand and pistol rose on the upswing, his fat finger pressed the trigger, unleashing a flash of white light. *Thwack!* The slug ricocheted off a steel joist in the bridge's underframe – and punched into Joe's left shoulder.

Joe reached for the entry wound with his right hand. His fingers were smeared in blood. He tested the quality of the injury by moving his left arm. He'd felt worse pain, and been more badly immobilised. He'd taken one for the team now, but that's all he was going to take from these pricks.

Lennie straightened his back against the wall and spat out scarlet. He stroked his jaw with his undamaged hand, false-yawning to see if anything was broken.

"OK, you clowns," said John. "Let's go."

"Where?" said Lennie, pleased that his jaw was working. He valued the ability to speak as much as he valued his eye-sight and hearing. The soupy stink of the Enoka's he could do without.

Joe clamped a hand to his shot shoulder to cap the bleeding, winking to Lennie that he too would survive into the next round.

"Your place," said John.

"We're not that stupid," said Lennie.

"Where then?" said John.

"There's a marina in Balmain. Safer than the bank. You won't find the coppers or the taxman floating a hundred metres offshore."

Lennie pushed himself up to standing. "Transport?"

"Our truck's round the corner," said John, waving his pistol. "You fuckin' turnips go first. Left out of the tunnel. You can test my aim if you want to try a runner."

Lennie and Joe walked side by side with the Enokas close behind. Lennie hobbled more than he needed to and held his hurt hand with his good one as if it needed a sling, which it didn't. Joe held his ripped shoulder, wondering if he could swing his good fist backward and clock two Enoka's for the price of one.

They walked from the tunnel up a quiet street of terrace houses to a parked white ute. Its driver's cabin had front and back seats, behind which there was a tray which had low side-walls and a dark tarpaulin clipped over the top.

Chris undid a couple of the tarp's elastic clips and reached inside the tray. He pulled out a filthy beach towel.

"Here," he said to Joe. "Mop ya-self up. I don't want ya bleedin' on my seats. Just bought this chariot."

Joe held the towel to his shot shoulder and then checked the towel for blood under a streetlight in the dusty gloom. Not too bad, he figured, the bullet had ripped through his shirt, skin, and a bit of muscle, but it had passed through without stopping or tearing a big vein or artery. He guessed the bullet's bounce off the steel joist had taken zing out of the slug before it hit him.

"Before we head off to your bank," said John. "You losers haven't seen our bro, Pago, have you?"

"Pago?" said Lennie. "Na. Is he lost?"

"Tell you what," said John. "We can have a longer chat about that later. Chris and I have a little questionnaire for the three of you."

"Three?" said Lennie.

Chris unclipped more of the tarp and threw a corner back. "You know this sheila, don't ya?"

Joe and Lennie peered into the back of the ute. Their eyes adjusted to the dim light. TC stared up at them. He had a gag in his mouth, one of those things with a rubber ball and leather straps. He was wearing pale boxer shorts and a matching T-shirt. His hands were tied behind his back and roped close to his tied ankles, forcing his body into a belly-out U-shape.

God, thought Lennie, it appeared the Enokas had carried the little bugger around by his tied wrists and ankles as if the rope was a carry strap. Poor TC had been turned into a designer handbag for lunatics.

Chris opened the back door of the twin cabin Toyota Hilux. He reached into a toolbox that was on the seat and extracted an electric drill which had a pencil-sized bit fixed in its mouth. He pressed the trigger and spun the bit.

"Let's see how we go at your marina, bro's. If we're happy, we're happy. If we're not happy, you can have a chat to the Interrogator here." Chris squeezed the trigger again, giggling.

Chris put his drill and toolbox in the back tray alongside TC and re-clipped the tarp. He walked around and climbed into the driver's seat.

John waved his gun, indicating for his hostages to get in. Joe climbed into the front passenger's seat. Lennie began to climb into the back seat directly behind the driver.

John grizzled to Lennie: "Do I look like a fuckwit to you?"

Lennie was burning to say "Yes". But he turned up his hands and gestured that he didn't get the point.

"Slide across, dick-nose," John said, forcing Lennie along the seat so that Lennie ended up sitting behind Joe. John took the seat behind his brother so he could keep his gun trained on his captives – and protect his brother's back.

The dust cloud over the city showed little sign of lifting as Lennie directed the Enokas to a small, harbour-side park in Balmain.

They pulled into a parking area atop a high cliff overlooking a swimming pool called the Dawn Fraser, named after a former Olympic swimmer who was as feisty as she was fast. The pool was built out into the jellyfish-rich harbour water and enclosed by timber-plank clad dressing sheds and expansive wood decks that were great for sunbaking and perving upon humanity in all its shapes and sizes and mental conditions.

Tonight, it was impossible to see much through the dust, but Lennie and Joe were pretty sure that small motorboats and yachts were moored as usual outside the pool.

"Got a pair of bolt cutters?" Lennie said as the group of four gathered beside the ute.

"Why?" said John.

"Need to cut a chain."

Chris shuffled in the back of his ute and found a battery-powered angle grinder. The four men walked down a steep bitumen path between thin strips of native bush and stringy trees onto a patch of manicured grass beside the water. Dinghies and kayaks stood on their tails in metal racks beside a sandstone-fringed slipway that inclined from dry land into the water.

"What the hell?" said John, pointing his pistol at Lennie. "What sort of marina is this?"

"A little one," said Lennie, pointing into the harbour. "We take a dinghy out to our buoy over there."

"And then?"

"We haul up the stash."

"If you're taking the piss," said Chris. "The Interrogator will be turning your balls into Swiss Cheese."

"Understood," said Lennie, who shuddered at the mention of cheese and balls. He wondered what terrible things lurked in the pink and purple folds he imagined dangling between the Enokas' legs.

"We'll use that one over there," Lennie said, pointing at wooden rowboat standing in the rack.

Joe pointed at a timber staircase that zig-zagged up a nearby sandstone cliff to a higher street. "The oars are tucked behind those steps."

Minutes later, the boat was unchained due to the efforts of Chris with the angle-grinder. The vessel floated in shallow water at the start of the slipway.

"This is crazy," said John. "This tub's gonna sink with four of us in there."

"Na," said Lennie, who was thigh-deep in water steadying the boat. "We just need to get the seating plan right."

The rowboat had one seat at the squared-off back, a wider middle seat for the rower, or rowers, and a narrower seat at the pointy end.

"How about this?" said Lennie. "Joe and I take an oar each and sit in the middle. Johnny, you sit in the back 'cause you are the biggest. And Chrissy goes up front."

John shook his head: "How about this? You row. I sit in the back and keep you honest. Christo and Red stay here on the shore."

"That might work if you hadn't smashed my hand. And then you busted Joe by shooting him in the shoulder. So what you've got now are two, one-armed men – and a rowboat that needs two oars to make it go."

John scratched his temple with the nose of the gun, trying to fathom Lennie's analysis, his fat finger sitting chock-a-block inside the trigger guard. Lennie thought about yelling: "Boo!"

Lennie said, "And I'll give you another tip: if you leave Joe here with Chrissy guarding him with that pissy little angle grinder, that'd be downright reckless on your part."

"I can fix that fuckin' problem right now," said John. "I'll shoot Red in the head."

"Sure. You can do that," said Lennie. "And then I won't get in the boat, and you won't get the stash."

"Oh, for fuck's sake," said John. "Let's all get in the boat."

Chris's face took on the look of a puzzled kid. He squeaked, "So what's underneath the buoy exactly?"

Lennie put his hands up in surrender. "Look...we've got a waterproof box out there on the end of the chain. There's gold bullion and cash. And a very nice handgun. A gold-plated Browning like Saddam Hussein used to have."

Chris made an O-shape with his lips and whistled. "O-kay!"

Lennie wondered if Chris had suffered permanent concussive brain damage, as well as a busted voice box, in his childhood play with his brothers.

With the boat in the shallows of the slipway, and the oars laid inside it, John insisted on climbing in first and taking pole position at the front. He had to be lifted and pushed in by Lennie and Joe, as Chris stood calf-deep in the water and pointed the gun.

With John seated – and back in command of the gun – Lennie and Joe got in. Chris pushed the boat out until the water was up to his thighs. The back-end of the boat dipped briefly below sea level as Chris rolled like a massive seal over the gunwale. He lay on his back on the floor, panting, mingled with Lennie's and Joe's feet.

Eventually, the men found balance by arranging themselves, as Lennie advised, into "the four points of a stretched diamond". Lennie and Joe, in order to pull the oars, had their backs to John and their faces to Chis who covered most of the back seat with his giant bum.

"Rowing is such a backward craft," said Lennie, pulling an oar in one-handed synchronicity with Joe.

"What are you on about?" said John.

"You know, the way you sit with your back facing where you're going...so you're looking into your past, unable to see your future."

"You're a weirdo," said John.

"You should think about it," said Lennie, who immediately regretted giving John clues about what was coming. He changed tack. "So when did you blokes decide joining Islamic State was a good idea?"

"You are talking out of your arse," John growled.

"Come on, mate," said Lennie. "I'm guessing you got hooked-up through that Iraqi mob your brothers got snug with inside Cell Block E. I remember when Jona and Toku got themselves those little prayer hats and mats to kneel on so they could point their bums away from Mecca."

"Just row the boat you racist cunt."

"Nothing racist about it, Johnny. Everyone's got to draw a line somewhere. I would have thought cutting someone's throat because they're taking their kids to school was a stretch, even for you."

"We're not doing that shit."

"You're aiding and abetting."

"Fuck you and your lawyer talk."

"So what are doing?"

"Getting the money you bastards thieved."

"Thieved," said Lennie. "That's an interesting word coming from your lips."

He thought about telling the Enokas that he and Joe had already "redistributed" most of the banknotes that rained over them at the wharf. The residents at Pauline's women's refuge got some, and so did some clients of a thieving accountant they'd dealt with. And yeah, they'd splashed out on giving the *Flamingo* a paint job and a new anchor. But, Lennie thought, that charity stuff with the women's safe house was bragging talk and it was likely to make the Enokas think there was less on the seabed below them, and that might upset the plan that was going OK so far. He elbowed Joe gently, and having gained his attention, nodded at Joe's chest.

Joe kept rowing with his good arm, and used the hand on the end of his throbbing other to reach into the front pocket of his check flannel shirt. He plucked out a ready-rolled joint of Mars Grass which he held aloft. "Anyone got a light?"

The Enokas liked to smoke weed, Lennie and Joe knew that from their prior dealings with the bros. And John, in particular, liked to yap and get expansive when he was on the gear.

"Over here," John said.

Joe swivelled to face John who was holding a plastic cigarette lighter. Joe offered him the unlit joint.

"Do I look that dumb, ranga boy?" said John, who grinned like he was the cleverest man in town. "You can be the king's taster."

Joe plugged the joint in his mouth and John lit it. Joe took a short drag and offered it to the Samoan. John waited briefly for the taster's reaction, and when he didn't go into convulsions, John snatched the joint. He toked hard. Then again, and again, locking smoke in his lungs.

"Hoy!" yelled Chris.

Joe relayed the joint to Chris.

John exhaled. "When we get your cash, all we're gonna do is buy cars. Been doing it for years."

Lennie turned his head towards John, who was scratching an ear with the nostril of the gun. Lennie was a split second from violently rocking the boat when John pointed his pistol into the murky sky and spoke.

"Was a time when all we did was buy trucks like our new Hilux up there on the hill. But these days we mostly do luxury shit like Maseratis and BMW's and Range Rovers."

Lennie took the dwindling joint from Chris and relayed it to John. He and Joe resumed rowing.

Lennie said, "So you've got a big garage at home, hey?"

"Na, we're not as stupid as you." John blew smoke. "We got a business model."

"Yeah? What sort?"

"Easier than shelling peas," said John. "We just get given cash to buy cars from different dealers in Melbourne, Sydney, or Timbuk-fucking-tu for all we care. Cash is king and it keeps its mouth shut. We give the motors to a guy who ships 'em overseas. To fuckin' Turkey or Pakistan...even the Philippines and Indonesia these days. Then some other mad fuckers sell them to rich generals or businessmen. If that cash, or those cars, turn into guns, it's nothing to do with us."

Lennie's brow furrowed. He figured John was only spilling the beans on his business because he was going to kill him and Joe when he got what he was after. The man was a bragger, always had been. "So what happened to the Hilux business?"

Chris squeaked, "They're still popular, but you want beater-uppers these days."

"Beater-uppers?" said Lennie, passing the dregs of the joint back to Chris.

Chris huffed and puffed. "You *are* as dumb as you look, Lennie. How else are the bro's gonna head for the hills with the Yanks and the Ruskies raining hell on 'em?"

"Enlighten me."

"For fuck's sake, you just shave ya beard, wear an *I Love Planet Earth* T-shirt, fill ya bashed-up truck with goats and kids – shove some diamonds up the kids' bums, or up the goats' – and tell the border guards you're runnin' from the baddies. Across you go with a bag a loot into a new life."

John chimed in. "There's ancient artefacts too. A decent religious statue is worth a bomb."

"Very sweet," acknowledged Lennie. "You guys are real specials. No doubt this Sunday, you'll strum ukuleles in your mum's Christian church singing Rock of Ages, and then nip around the corner to your IS mates to pick up the contract for your next job and earn a nice little commish. Like that truck up there, hey?"

Chris scowled. "We're not racist like you, Lennie. We've done jobs for your mob too."

"What mob's that?"

"White rednecks who want a new world order."

"That's a worthy cause," Lennie replied. "Some neo-Nazis hire you to knock off a gun shop, hey?'

"Shut the fuck up," John growled. "Where's this buoy?"

"Here," said Lennie, tapping the tip of his oar on a floating, orange and white painted, lifesaver ring.

In the dust and dim light, it had taken him a while to find the one he was after. Loose lips sink ships, Lennie reminded himself without speaking, and if your ship sinks, you better be able to swim. He knew from prison that none of the Enokas had ever learned to swim. They were a family of waders.

"OK," said John, waving his gun. "Haul the box up."

Lennie pointed at his smashed hand. Joe stroked his shot shoulder.

"You need one man with two hands to pull up a chain," said Lennie. "Otherwise we'll tip this boat for sure."

"Christo," said John. "You're on."

Lennie and Joe used their oars to manoeuvre the back of the dinghy toward the floating ring so Chris could grab the chain.

This ring, from Lennie's and Joe's maritime experience, would likely be anchored by a chain to a massive block of concrete sitting on the harbour bed. The chain may, alternatively, be attached to a steel peg that had been rammed into the seabed with a jackhammer. Either way, it would take a tug-of-war team on a massive vessel to break that chain from its underwater mooring.

"Holy Moses," said Chris, pulling so hard on the chain that the dinghy dipped and took in water.

"There's a lotta gold in that box," Lennie explained. "We usually have a winch and a bigger boat. Here, I've still got one good hand."

As Lennie moved off his seat to assist Chris, the boat rocked violently. He sat down to re-balance the craft.

"Joe," said Lennie. "You'll have to counter my weight as I move."

Joe pulled his oar from its rowlock, grasped its pole midpoint with his good hand, and prepared to stand.

Lennie called: "On the count of three. One, two..."

Joe bent at the knees for balance and power – and rammed the grip-end of his oar backward, smashing the tip into John's nose where it glanced sideways and ripped into an eye socket. John groaned and reeled.

Chris, blind to the hit on his brother, was still bum-up gripping the chain with both hands, his head and shoulders hanging over the water, eyes fixed on the prospect of treasure. Lennie gripped the gunwale beside his seat for leverage – and heel-kicked Chris's rump. The big man began tipping. Lennie kicked him again, and again; sinking his foot into the pillow of flesh; shifting his shots from bum-cheek to bum-cheek: Chris tumbled headfirst into the drink.

John, clutching his bloodied eye with one hand, swung his barrel towards Joe who crashed the stump of his oar into John's other eye. Gunfire flashed. Joe flipped his oar over, grasping it like a lance, and jabbed the blade-end into John's throat. The big Samoan gasped. Joe flipped the oar and batted the stump against John's face; John tipped sideways out of the boat. But as he rolled out, he threw his free hand at the gunwale, catching its edge with his fingers. His gun came up over the side and unleashed a burst of light and explosive clap.

Joe didn't wait to see if he'd been hit; he kneeled and grabbed the hot barrel of the gun, pointing its nose skyward.

Lennie, seeing Joe's move, looked at Chris whose flailing arms were churning foam beside the dinghy. Chris's head slipped beneath the surface.

Joe reached with his spare hand for a steel-bladed anchor on a chain that was under the front seat. Sitting on the middle seat, he hammered John's fingers using the gunwale as an anvil. John yelped and let go of the boat. But he wouldn't let go of the gun.

Joe tightened his grip on the barrel and chopped John's gun-toting wrist with the anchor. The howling bull released and his body slipped into the water.

Lennie poked his oar's blade to where the top of Chris's head was just visible under the surface. The desperate man grabbed the blade. Lennie hauled; Chris's head spluttered above the waterline.

Chris gasped. "Can't...swim. *We* can't swim."

"That's a shame," said Lennie, perching on the middle seat and holding his oar with Chris clutching the end of it. "See that round thing next to you? It's called a lifesaver. Grab it."

"I can't."

"Your choice," said Lennie, who ripped his slippery blade from Chris's grasp.

Chris flailed and threw a hand at the ring – which was less than an arm's length away. His fingers caught hold of it.

Lennie said to Joe, "How's Johnnie's swimming lesson going?"

Joe looked over his side of the boat. "I think he needs a snorkel." Joe sat on the middle seat next to Lennie.

Joe held his oar's blade above the water where bubbles were rising. "Got a bite," he said and pulled John and his head above the surface. The big man gasped.

Joe was grateful that saltwater gave bodies buoyancy because John's mass was so immense it threatened to tip Joe from the boat. "You pull too hard, and I let it go!" Joe said firmly. "Now, if you stay calm, I'm gonna drag you around so you can join your bro hanging onto that lifesaver. OK?"

John whimpered as Joe dragged him slowly, for there was no other speed to be had, around the side of the boat towards Lennie, who took the oar and guided John next to his brother who clung to the ring like the love of his life.

John claimed a piece of the ring. The combined weight of the brothers trying to get all they could of their bodies onto the buoy pushed it under the surface.

Lennie moved to the back seat of the boat and shook his head. "You can't sit on the thing! Hang on to it, but keep your bodies in the water. And kick your feet a little. Capiche?"

The Enokas slid off the ring and held the float by their fingers, kicking like kids at the edge of a pool.

Joe, positioning himself in the middle seat of the dinghy, rowed a couple of body length's from the Enokas to remove from them the temptation to lunge at the craft. He pulled the oars in and laid them on the floor of the boat; a black wallet sat beside his boot. He picked it up and opened the Velcro seal. He waved John Enoka's photo driver's licence at Lennie, then a credit card. He handed the wallet to Lennie.

"Whacko!" said Lennie, flicking through the contents. "This is worth its weight in gold...what sort of boofhead keeps his PIN numbers and passwords on a piece of paper?"

"Let's get out of here," said Joe.

Lennie called to the Enokas, "Now you boys enjoy each other's company – we're off."

Chris wailed. "You can't leave us here. I'm havin' a heart attack!"

"Don't you worry, Chrissy" said Lennie. "We're going to send someone for you. But it won't be an ambulance, so you better save that cardiac arrest."

"Let's make a deal!" squealed Chris.

"Here's the deal," said Lennie, "We just found Johnny's wallet. His life's story is in there. Even your mum's address. So if you mention our names to anyone, and we mean anyone – or you come near me and Joe again, or any of our friends – we won't leave you with a lifebuoy to cling to. Comprende?"

"Who's coming for us?" said John.

"Let's not spoil the surprise," said Lennie.

Joe re-slotted the oars and started for shore.

"Sure you're OK doing that?" Lennie asked, as the Samoans faded into the mist.

"I've had worse bites from bigger dogs."

Lennie swivelled his head back in the direction of the Enokas who were yelling: "Help! Help!"

Lennie wiggled a tooth that had been loosened by the earlier smack in the face with the gun, and tasted blood. He cupped his hands to make a megaphone and called into the murk. "Don't make any noise or thrash about. There're bull sharks out here – and they'll tear your bums off like its fairy floss."

The Enokas went silent.

2 - BARBED WIRE BEAR

AS THEY REACHED THE SHORELINE, spits of rain mixed with dust in the air to run dark rivulets down their faces. To Lennie, Joe's camouflage-patterned face looked fit for a Vincent Van Gough portrait. Joe thought Lennie's face needed a wash.

Without speaking, they put the dinghy in the storage rack, the oars behind the steps, and trudged uphill to where the Enokas' truck was parked.

They peeled back the tarp: TC's doe-like eyes peered up at them. They unstrapped his ball-gag and found a cutter in the toolbox to sever his ropes.

It took several minutes and a massage from Joe for the chemist's muscles to regain sufficient blood flow for him to straighten his limbs. Joe lifted him out of the tray and placed his feet on the ground, wrapping an arm around TC's little body to stop him from collapsing.

Rain showered.

Lennie cupped his hands until they were filled and washed his face and rinsed his cut mouth. Joe took his shirt off and let the rain wash his shot shoulder. TC leaned against the side of the truck and stared into space and the falling droplets. The trio felt time passing but they were in no rush to catch it.

Lennie broke the spell. "How much cooking time do you reckon?" he said, stretching his neck and shoulders and massaging his eyes with clenched fists as if he was waking from a deep sleep.

"It'll be daylight in about five hours," said Joe.

Lennie stroked his chin. "Mm...we want these bastards to shiver and shake, but it won't help anyone if we don't get them plucked from the water breathing. And we don't want them plucked by fishermen. It's nearly midnight. Let's make it three hours then."

"Why leave them breathing?" said TC.

"So we can stuff up their mates," said Lennie.

"What mates?" said TC, who opened the back door of the truck's cabin and plucked the electric drill from the toolbox on the seat. He squeezed the trigger and gave The Interrogator a spin. "Let's give them a taste of their own medicine, as you guys like to say."

Joe liked it that TC was regaining spunk, but this wasn't the time to go headless-chook trying to dish out revenge. "There's a bigger picture tonight," he said to TC.

"What picture?" said TC, the weight of the drill forcing his arm to drop by his side. The Interrogator whirred furiously, threatening to bore a hole in TC's bare left foot.

Joe shook his head. "Trust us."

TC used both hands to put the drill back in the box.

Lennie massaged his brow and sighed. "Our prints are all over this truck. So we have one last job, boys."

They ripped up a T-shirt that was in a bag in the back seat, and dipped the rags in petrol from a can they found in the tray. The trio cleaned their fingerprints, footprints, dripped blood, and hopefully their DNA, off the upholstery and paintwork. They did so because Lennie was pretty sure that in the not too distant future, law enforcement officials from a variety of departments would be crawling all over the truck.

They walked uphill and across a park to a street lined by terrace houses that were many times larger than any in their own neighbourhood. Drunks were returning home after nights out, so the bedraggled trinity didn't have to wait long for vacated taxis. One headed towards them. But it accelerated on approach and shot past. As soon as the next empty taxi caught them in its headlights, it whizzed past too.

Lennie chuckled, the obvious dawning on him. "We look shiftier than a car with ten gears."

Joe looked at barefoot TC with his wet fringe now fallen over his forehead. His rain-soaked white T-shirt and matching shorts appeared glued to his childlike frame. "TC, you know you could pass for a girl."

"No, please," TC protested.

"We can't walk home," said Lennie, hamming up the hobble from his bruised knee. "Look at us. Circus freaks. Mental patients. Take your pick. The coppers would have us cuffed before we hit the main road."

TC grumbled, but he did as directed and stood on his own by the curb looking as cute and lost as he could. Lennie and Joe lurked behind a tree...

A sedan car, displaying probationary driver's plates, stopped. The front passenger window motored down. "Need a lift?" the lone, young male driver asked.

TC bowed his head.

"I won't bite," said the driver, who leaned across and pushed the passenger door open. "I'll take you wherever you want."

Lennie darted from behind the tree and jumped in, winking at the young man who gobbled like a goldfish. While the kid blinked, trying to grasp what was happening, TC and Joe slipped into the back seat and closed the door.

Lennie smiled. "Thought your luck was in, did you? You find this little girl. Out on her own in the dark of night. Easy pickings, hey?"

"Naa. 'course not," said the kid, who blushed pink.

"Tell you what," said Lennie. "There's fifty bucks in it, if you take us across town."

The kid had a quick think. "Show me the dough," he demanded, apparently sensing the balance of power was swinging his way.

Joe said from behind him. "Tell you what, clever Trevor. You can travel in your trunk, or you can drive and earn a fee."

"I'll drive. No problems."

Lennie rubbed his chin. "Mm. Just in case there are problems, give me your wallet. And your phone."

"Are you gonna kill me?" said the kid, shaking.

"Depends," said Lennie.

The kid's lip quivered.

"Oh, for God's sake," said Lennie, accepting that his sense of humour might have gone on the blink. "Maybe it's best if you do ride in the boot."

"Na," said the kid, bug-eyed. "I'm good." He hastily handed over his wallet and phone.

Lennie opened the wallet and examined the driver's licence inside it. "*Richard Face*. Your parents like a laugh, did they?"

"Huh?" said the kid.

"Listen, Dick," said Lennie, studying the kid's button nose and deciding he was probably teased to hell at school. "Turn right at the end of the street."

"My name is Rick," the kid insisted.

"Of course it is," said Lennie. As the car took off, he turned to TC: "Given the circumstances, I reckon you should stay with us, until the dust settles."

Joe looked out the blurred windows. "It's settlin' pretty fast. This rain is bucketing."

TC massaged jaw muscles that had been strained by the ball gag. "Thanks. I'd like that."

*

"Pull over here thanks, *Rick*," said Lennie.

The kid stopped kerbside a street away from Lennie's and Joe's home. The rain was clearing. Lennie gave the kid a fifty-dollar note.

"Can I have my phone and wallet?" the kid asked.

"Sure," said Lennie, who took his own phone from his jeans pocket and photographed the kid's driver's licence, and his bank card and a student ID. In the glove box, Lennie found the car's insurance and registration documents. He photographed them too.

"Listen, Rick Face," said Lennie, "Maybe you're a lovely young man who drives around late at night looking for young women in distress to rescue. Or maybe you're a serial killer, paedophile, or rapist. Even a combo, perhaps. We're too tired right now to give you a proper grilling."

The kid's lip quivered.

"Whatever you are," said Lennie, "we know where you live now, and how to find you. And you wouldn't want a late-night visit from us, would you? So here's some free advice: You didn't see us, and we didn't see you. OK?"

The trembling driver nodded.

As the kid's car disappeared, TC crumbled, fainting on a footpath. Joe, despite his shot shoulder, gave TC a piggy-back for the final stretch home.

Rawcus went into a squawking spin when they opened the front door and stepped inside. "Whaat time d'ya call this! Whaat time d'ya call this!"

"Sorry," said Joe, who spoke cockatoo better than Lennie and had long been the primary medium between Rawcus and the human world. "We're home now. OK?"

They dressed their wounds, put on clean, warm clothes, and took beers and a couple of blocks of milk chocolate into the back garden. The sky was clear of dust after being washed by the rain which had moved on too. The sight of a crisp half-moon was worth tucking into, the trio of friends agreed, especially after a few tokes of Mars Grass.

After a while sky-gazing, Lennie said, "It's 1am. I'm going to get some z's. I'll set my alarm and make the call at three o'clock."

Joe set TC up with pillows and blankets on the sofa. Rawcus kept TC company by using an armrest as a perch. The bird was asleep in about a minute, standing as always.

Rawcus's breathing rattled with irritating predictability.

"Just poke him with this if you can't bear the snoring," said Joe, handing TC a bamboo chopstick. "He's got a few years on the clock so he gets cranky easily. His beak'll chop a finger off, if you're not careful. Especially one of those little pegs of yours, TC."

TC looked nervous.

Joe winked. "It wouldn't go to waste. Lennie could turn it into a lucky Jack."

*

Lennie's phone alarm sounded with a chorus of bleating sheep.

He dressed and took a phone handset from a box under his bed, along with a battery and a SIM card. He put the pieces separately into his jeans pockets, along with a Jack that had a violet-coloured fingernail. After checking that Joe, TC, and Rawcus were safely sleeping, he slipped quietly out the front door.

He headed back to the railway underpass where the encounter with the Enokas had occurred. Lennie figured that if anyone else was going to be loitering under the bridge at 3am, they'd have to be weirder than him, which shrunk the potential candidates pretty close to nil. But just in case there *were* weirder characters than him floating around, he had stuffed John Enoka's pistol, which had a couple of bullets left, in the back waistband of his jeans.

As he walked, the gun went from feeling cold to feeling uncomfortable slotted between his bum cheeks. While this holstering technique was popular on TV, he wondered how many real bad arses used it – and if they did, how often they shot themselves in the bum or spine and became paralysed. He thought about stuffing it down the front of his jeans, but this might shoot his cock off, especially if the safety catch was unreliable. He transferred the gun to his hand.

His skin prickled then burned; it felt like he was being hugged from behind by a bear made of barbed wire. He dragged the beast along and wondered why the possibilities of existence were as endless as they were pointless in so many ways.

For example, what was the point of being able to have the idea – in other words, to be able *to think* – that Rawcus could transform into a man, and Lennie into a bird, when the likelihood of that actually happening, as Joe keeps telling him, is so near zero you'd have to travel beyond the edge of the universe to even get close to the number that flashes to the right side of the decimal point in Joe's brain whenever he considers Lennie's question about his and Rawcus's shape-shifting prospects.

Lennie walked on and with great effort side-stepped this birdman conundrum. But his thoughts immediately landed inside a sticky possibility that the electrical energy being generated by his furious thinking might cause his brain to explode, or implode, or melt like bad electrical wiring. The barbed-wire bear's hug tightened on his back. Lennie realised what was happening...

"Hello, Mr Psychosis," he snarled out loud to the prickly beast. "Now. I'm going to say this once, as nicely as I can: Get your hands off me. Fuck! Off!"

The beast just grinned and hung on tight.

Where was Joe when he needed him? Lennie looked around the empty street in a city of millions. There was no-one who could help him. Ultimately, there never was, and never would be. Physical action, he thought, that's always the best way to stuff-up the beast: focus on the outside world.

Lennie saw that he had landed at his destination under the brick arch. He put the battery and SIM card in the phone and dialled an anonymous-caller hotline that connected him to the Australian Federal Police.

"Hello, old chap," Lennie said, practising his accent and tone while the phone dialled. "Hello, old chap."

He'd been learning what he had dubbed *toff-speak* using YouTube videos of Prince Charles of Wales rabbiting on about architecture and flowers. A man's voice answered the hotline.

Lennie said, "Please, do listen very carefully young man, and turn your recording thingy on."

"Can I have your name please, sir?" the hot-liner said.

"You can call me Father Bird."

"Are you a man of religion?"

"I am calling *about* a matter of religion, in a roundabout way."

"You have called the Australian Federal Police, sir. If you have spiritual or mental health issues, I can give you more appropriate numbers to dial."

Lennie countered: "Are you interested in persons engaged in fundraising for violent extremists?"

"Yes. What can you tell us?"

"There are two men currently clinging to a lifebuoy in Sydney Harbour."

Father Bird proceeded to spell the names of the floating men and provide colourful physical descriptions. He added that the men were related to two brothers who had died – one of self-inflicted shotgun wounds, and the other from a cardiac arrest triggered by a snakebite and a fatty diet – while fleeing the federal police on another matter. Lennie then dictated the registration details of Chris Enoka's ute, including its location.

"My strong advice to you and your colleagues," said Father Bird, "is that you *do not* take these men in for questioning. More precisely, I advise that you be most careful not to raise their suspicions that intelligence organisations such as yours are interested in them at all. You should confine yourselves to a pure, humanitarian rescue operation this morning – it's probably wise, therefore, to send the Water Police – and then wish the men good health and bade them on their way."

"Please go on, Father Bird."

"I may not need to tell you this, because you sound like a bright young fellow, but for the avoidance of confusion, I will. I believe that if you install a tracking device in the shiny new vehicle they are driving and follow these men, they will lead you to an extremist network that is raising black money in Australia, including from armed robbery and drug dealing and protection rackets, and shipping it overseas to finance radical jihad against our own armed forces and our allies.

"And now that the Western coalition and Russian military, among others, have apparently broken the Islamic State Caliphate in Syria and Iraq, no doubt these funds – which are disguised and transported in the form of luxury cars – will be diverted to other extremist projects in territories closer to our homes. The Philippines, for example, or Indonesia.

"How do you know this, Father Bird, about these men of yours?"

"They made a confession to me."

"I understood men like you never revealed the contents of confessions. Are you an ethical person, Father Bird?"

"That is a very large question for so early in the morning. And I have not had coffee, or hard liquor, which normally assist me with that type of rumination at this hour. So back to business: I suggest you despatch the regular police forthwith to the location I have just given you, armed with the background and tactics I have outlined. In the meantime, I will consider the question of my personal ethics which you have raised."

Lennie paused. "Oh, a final point. These men I believe have a freelance mentality."

"Freelance?"

"They will work for the highest bidder. Wouldn't surprise me that if some neo-Nazis knocked on their door, they'd assist them to raise funds and acquire weapons too. For a fee. But I must go. You'll be tracing the location of this call, of course."

"Please, don't hang up."

"Toodle-oo."

Father Bird dismantled his phone, transformed back into Lennie Larsen, and began walking home. Lennie sensed the prickly bear following him, but he could neither see, nor feel, nor hear the beast anymore and this pleased him.

3 - ARTISTS

IN THE MORNING, Lennie, TC, and Joe sat in the back garden around the table drinking tea and coffee and smoking. Rawcus looked on from a perch on the top of the paling fence. TC tapped ash from a rollie onto the courtyard paving.

"You grub!" called Rawcus.

"Sorry," said TC, who bent down and tried to pick up the grey crumbs.

Lennie and Joe smiled at Rawcus's impersonation of Lennie's gran in her prime.

Rawcus, given his elevated vantage point, was first to see the human head rise behind the back fence. "Giss a kiss, love!" he screeched at the peeper.

The bird's companions followed his amorous gaze to where the head bobbed.

Lennie concluded that the man who owned the head was either very tall, or he was standing on a box in the laneway, or he was employing a height-lifting device such as platform shoes. The upper parts of his suit jacket, shirt, and tie were visible. He had a round, pink face that appeared to be about

50 years of age, and his head was frighteningly well-coifed with straw-coloured hair.

"Excuse me gents," called the man. "Am I speaking with Mr Leonard Larson and Mr Joseph Clarke."

"Nup," said Lennie, unable to take his eyes off the man's bouffant, ruling out extreme mental illness and deciding the guy was a toss-up between a TV reporter and a real estate agent. He also resembled an American President he'd seen on the news, but this laneway guy's skin wasn't as orange.

Joe said, "Take your Peeping Tom act somewhere else. Father Dominic sunbakes nude a couple of doors up behind the church and he likes an audience."

The man shook his head, apparently puzzled, but didn't back down.

"Listen, mate! We're not selling!" called Lennie, who decided the guy was in real estate. The shiny-suited twats were always trying to get them to sell.

The man replied, "My name is Detective Sergeant Bob Swain. I need to talk with Mr Larson and Mr Clarke about a criminal investigation."

"Faark," Lennie hissed, spilling his tea as he sat up straight. A roll call began scrolling inside his skull like captions on a TV screen: Pago Enoka, Chris Enoka, John Enoka, filmmaker Toby Runyon, serial killer Ken Milan, fake constable Robbie Hogg and his dead mate Arty. And that was just a recent list.

"What investigation might that be?" said Lennie.

"Can I come in?" the detective said. "I feel like a dickhead standing on a milk crate, yelling over a fence."

"Feel like?" Lennie muttered to his companions. They chuckled. Regaining his composure, Lennie called to the man, "Do you have a warrant?"

"I hope it won't come to that. My colleague has been knocking on your front door. I thought I'd try the lane. Our inquiry is in relation to the apprehension of Kenneth Milan. I know that Mr Larsen and Mr Clarke had an encounter with him a few nights ago. We are trying to join some dots."

Lennie nodded at TC to come closer, then whispered. "Mate, stuck on the fridge door, there's a card with Pauline Gerrity's number on it. Give her a call, tell her we have these visitors and get her to put our lawyer on standby. But ask her to hold the cavalry charge until these meter maids here break cover and we know what their angle is."

TC winked. "Don't want to look like you've got anything to hide, hey?" He stood and went inside.

"What's she up to?" called the detective.

"Putting the kettle on," said Lennie. "Give me a sec and I'll find the key to the gate...do you know where it is, Joe?"

Joe stood and slowly turned his shorts pockets out. "It's here somewhere."

"Gents," said the detective, raising his voice. "This is a serious criminal matter that's not for public consumption. I can't conduct inquiries over a bloody fence!"

"Hold your horses, mate," Lennie replied. Employing his best magician's sleight of hand, he took a packet of Mars Grass from his back pocket and hid it under the leaves of a pot plant beside the table. But there wasn't much he could do about the spare bedroom upstairs which was harbouring a small jungle of floor-to-ceiling hydroponic marijuana. This might be his and Joe's last moment of freedom for a fairly long time, so he was keen to suck on it a little longer.

TC appeared in the kitchen doorframe and gave Lennie a thumbs-up.

Lennie called, "Kettle's boiled detective. Joe, would you help TC make a fresh brew, and let Detective Swain's mate in the front door?"

Lennie stepped slowly to the gate, pulled a key from his pocket, and un-padlocked the bolt. "Come in."

*

The five men sat around the kitchen table holding a variety of tea and coffee mugs in a variety of ways.

Joe wasn't risking any of the vintage Royal Doulton china on them, given he'd calculated a 50:50 chance of armed combat erupting. Due to this delicate balance, he made an executive decision to hold off on popping into Detective Swain's and Detective Tony Corleone's coffees the sedative crumbs disguised as sugar granules that TC had ground up while talking to Pauline. Joe would wait until the nature of the detectives' inquiries became clearer.

Lennie glanced at the winking green light of a micro-camera that was permanently rigged in the centre of the ceiling. His invention was designed to look like a fire alarm and it did a passable job. On this occasion, he wanted to make sure that anything big-haired Bob and suntanned Tony said was properly recorded and preserved for possible defence purposes.

Rawcus eyed the human assembly from his swinging rod that was roped to the ceiling in a corner of the room. "Watch him!" he cried to no-one in particular.

Detective Bob glanced up, bug-eyed, his right hand grabbing the grip of a pistol that was holstered on his belt. "Watch who?" said the lawman, his eyes darting around the kitchen.

Joe glared at Rawcus. "Ignore him, detective. He's just a trouble maker with a big mouth."

Rawcus turned his back on the humans and faced the wall.

"Is he sulking?" said Bob, who softened the hold on his gun handle.

"He'll be alright," said Joe.

Lennie said, "So, you want to talk about Ken Milan?"

"Watch him!" cried Rawcus, still facing the corner of the room.

Bob, who was sipping from his mug, stopped suddenly. He sniffed the contents. "What's in this?"

"Just coffee," Joe assured him, thinking that a jumpy copper and a loaded gun were not a good combo.

Bob put the cup down as if it might contain poison. "It's not public yet," he said. "but Milan murdered two people in the vicinity of your rural property, around the time you encountered him."

"What's that got to do with us?" said Lennie.

"Did you come across a pair of policemen – either on the way into, or out of your property that night – separate to meeting our task force that was chasing Milan?"

"No. Why do you ask?"

"About twenty-four hours after you gave our colleagues your account of meeting Milan, we found a man's naked body in a rural shed about an hour's drive from yours. He'd been killed with a single blow to the head with a small axe. That's what the forensics suggest. Another man was found in the shed. He had been strangled with barbed fencing wire. And he was dressed in a police uniform."

"How weird," Lennie said, rolling his eyes at Joe and TC who looked equally shocked.

"Thing is," said Bob. "The victims appear to have been posing as policemen."

"The plot thickens," said Lennie.

Joe put his head in his hands, clenching his teeth, worrying that Lennie might be laying it on too thick.

Bob resumed. "Milan has confessed to garrotting the man, and killing the other guy with an axe. But his description of the axe he used doesn't match the science on a couple of levels."

"Gosh!" said Lennie, cradling his chin with an open hand.

Bob went on. "Milan describes a full-blown axe, while the forensics suggests a smaller tool, like a tomahawk. But we have no actual weapon, nor a crime scene that fits an axe attack."

"Why would he spin a yarn like that?" said Lennie.

"He's the sort of lunatic who's after the body count. Notor-bloody-riety. Notches on the gun. He's already facing several life sentences for the previous murders, so maybe he can't see any downside. And it might inject a bit more fear into his future cellmates."

"Wikipedia," Lennie muttered.

"What?" said Bob.

Lennie was thinking that serial killers had some of the more interesting profiles on the online encyclopedia. Milan was probably trying to fatten his portfolio for history buffs. "You're smart guys. You'll work it out."

Joe was thinking that a tomahawk was sitting in a plastic bag in the garden shed with Robbie Hogg's fingerprints all over it. The words *slack* and *stupid* drifted inside his skull, bumping into each other like slapstick clowns. He'd been keeping it in case Robbie went weak at the knees and told the police about Mia.

Bob said, "This is where we need your help. The strangled man did some finger-painting on the shed floor with his own blood. In other words, he wasn't quite dead when Milan left him."

"Interesting painting?" said Lennie.

"He scratched a couple of triangular shapes that looked like lightning bolts. Ring a bell?"

"Too abstract for me...Joe?"

Joe nodded in agreement.

"It's not that abstract. It looked very much like the company logo that's painted on the Firefly Electrics van out in the street. That's your business, isn't it?"

Lennie sipped tea. "Milan nicked some of our promotional clothing that night. Your colleagues were witness to that. The dead guy must have seen the symbol on the shirt Milan was wearing."

"See, there's the rub," said Bob, looking Lennie in the eye, then at Joe. "Milan dumped every piece of that clothing of yours in a cabin on his way to the big shed where the bodies were found. He swapped clothes in that cabin, put on some old shorts, and an overcoat. So...if he arrives at the killing shed dressed like that, how would the dying man get inspired to paint a lightning bolt just like your business logo?"

"It's got me stuffed, Bob. What about you, Joe?"

Joe looked at the sugar jar with a top layer of TC's crushed sedatives, and then at a pick handle leaning in a corner of the room beside the fridge. He said, "Maybe the dead guy was into black magic or something? Wizards like triangles."

"I think you mean pentangles," said Bob.

"You're the expert," said Joe.

Bob looked at Joe like he was a moron. Bob said, "Milan also claims he buried another body on your property under some trees. In a sleeping bag. Do you mind if we send a team out to have a dig around?"

"Go for your lives, mate," said Lennie. "So how'd you catch him?"

"We nabbed him dressed in a fake police uniform driving a fake paddy wagon. He rolled the wagon taking a corner. Milan had been drinking some chemical in a brown bottle that we are still having analysed and checked for prints."

Lennie gulped.

"By the way," said Bob, scanning the battered and bruised trio he was talking to. "What happened to you lot? Looks like you've been hit by a truck."

Lennie chuckled. "Ha. We've been practising on each other for one of those black-tie charity boxing matches. To raise money for wayward youth. We've got our learner plates on in the ring, I'm afraid."

"Better learn how to duck, boys," said Bob. "And what about you, sweetheart?" he said to TC. "You're fighting out of your division, aren't you?"

TC's jaw was visibly bruised where the ball-gag strap had been. "I'm the trainer, detective. I stepped a bit close to a right cross. Won't happen again, I can assure you of that."

Bob and Tony did the TV copper routine and put their business cards on the kitchen table before they left, asking Lennie and Joe to call if anything occurred to them that might help solve the mystery.

After shutting the front door on the detectives, Lennie wiped the sweat from his brow with a kitchen towel and said, "Don't know about you guys, but I need to get out."

"Get out!" called Rawcus.

"Give me a minute," said Joe, who stepped outside to the garden shed and collected the tomahawk wrapped in its rubbish bag.

With Rawcus playing pirate-bird on Joe's shoulder, the three men walked from the garden into the back lane and headed uphill towards the local café strip. Lennie and Joe took turns explaining to TC their encounter with the fake cops and the Polish contortionists. As they approached the street, Joe tossed the bagged hawk into a builder's rubbish skip beside an idle construction site, reaching in to make sure it was covered with rubble.

As they walked away, Lennie said to Joe. "Mate, my finger-prints are on that ether bottle Robbie nicked, and that Milan picked up – and my prints are in the police database. I'm stuffed."

Joe grinned. He thought about playing a game but decided against it given the furrows on Lennie's brow. "Remember those rubber gloves I gave you to wear for the Kangaroo Court? You never touched that bottle."

Lennie went gobbling goldfish and high-fived Joe. As they walked, Lennie massaged his jaw in thought. "Was that escape by luck or design?"

"Don't overthink it," said Joe.

Rawcus shook his head. "Over-think it!"

Lennie touched the Jack in his pocket.

When they turned the corner into the main street, they were confronted by a newspaper poster wired to a power pole outside the local convenience store. It read: *Mystery: Judge's Son Hung by Who?*

Lennie went into the shop and stepped out moments later with a copy of the newspaper tucked under an arm. They walked along the local eating strip until Joe found an empty table outside a café that had chairs with backs to lean upon, and not an upturned milk crate in sight.

They ordered breakfast from a waiter with a snakeskin pattern tattooed all over his exposed forearms and who was wearing a bushranger-style beard, a white collarless shirt, and grey trousers held up by braces.

Lennie, inspired by the waiter's attire, was having visions of their recent action in the bush and Sid Nolan's Ned Kelly paintings, when his phone pinged.

He read the screen before handing it to Joe who grimaced as he deciphered each sentence: *Greetings from Poland. Hope ur good. We r. We have good news. Karl and me are invited to act at the Sydney Comedy Festival next year. R we safe to cum? Will you cum? Luv, Mia.*

While he was cock-a-hoop that the Poles were alive, Mia's note made Joe doubly determined to go to his next reading and writing lesson. He may have been a late starter with this stuff, but someone had to save proper English from dying out against attack from all this do-it-yourself shorthand.

Coffees arrived in the hands of the Ned Kelly impersonator. Lennie admired the young man's wavy dark hair and beard. Lennie thought that maybe it was time to ditch his own razors and get hairy again, not least because Father Francesco only appeared occasionally in his dreams these days, and mainly in cameo roles.

Lennie stirred his coffee and opened the newspaper. He scanned the story about the judge's son: it said that two nights ago, a forty-year-old man had been abducted by "unknown assailants". Toby Runyon had been encased in gaffer tape and hung from a tree by the two black-clad people who claimed they were installing street art for the city council.

Bystanders had whacked the wrapped man with sticks for over an hour, believing he was a mechanised dummy, while police watched on, until a caller to 000 said a real man was inside the cocoon. Runyon was the son of a Federal Court judge, whose family tree boasted generations of judges and lawyers whose roots could be traced back to the first settlement of Australia. Runyon's physical injuries would not result in permanent disablement, the newspaper said, but he had been hospitalised in a private psychiatric unit. Police were investigating emerging allegations of sexual assaults by Runyon upon female staff and child modelling clients in his film studio, triggered by the 000 caller identified only as *Audny*.

"You're in strife, Joe," said Lennie, looking up from the news pages.

"What sort?"

Lennie showed his companions a grainy, half-page photo of a dark, blob-shaped creature, cropped from one taken by a selfie-snapper. It accompanied a comment piece by the paper's arts editor about what the "artists" who hung Runyon were trying to say about contemporary society and the judicial system. The photo was captioned, *Wanted: FoFo.*

"Jesus, this guy's a babbler," said Lennie. "He's compared us to a British street artist called Banksy. And says FoFo might be a woman wearing a padded suit. To boot, the dickhead has called us *borderline psychos.*"

"Borderline?" said TC, rolling his eyes.

"Artists," Joe said softly, as if the description was worth framing.

"Arr-tists!" screeched Rawcus, shuffling along Joe's shoulder, whirling his head in circles as if the world was insane.

The End...for now

Thank you for reading *Kangaroo Court*, Book #2 in the *Firefly Electrics Series*.

In Book #3, *Galaxy Motel*:

Lennie, Joe, and Rawcus are haunted by underworld rumours that have linked them to a fortune, belonging to terrorists, which fell onto a city wharf during a cargo-loading accident.

When visitors carrying unusual tools, and wearing hardhats and sunglasses, knock on their front door, the trio needs to dance fast to avoid losing life or limb, or both. They enlist the help of a blow-up doll named Mavis, a homemade electric chair - and the Galaxy Motel.

Meanwhile, their childhood friend, Pauline Gerrity, needs assistance to deal with a professional man who has a keen eye for underage girls who reside at Pauline's refuge for abused mothers. They've dubbed the man Mr Teflon for good reason: he's a law enforcement insider. Could a fantastic trip to the beach enable them to rewire Mr T's soul and make the world safer?

One thing's for sure, Lennie, Joe, and Rawcus keep learning that the poet Robbie Burns got it right when he said "the best-laid plans of mice and men often go awry."

Learn more: www.markfurnessswriter.com

Other books by Mark Furness -

Under Eden, an international crime trilogy: #1 *The Ebola Conspiracy; #2 Freefall; #3 Redbox*

Justice Machine, Book #1 in the *Firefly Electrics Series*.

Short stories -

The Trespasser: Tale of a Digital Peeping Tom.

Drink with a Stranger: Journey to the Bizarre in Delhi, India.

Hugo's Awakening: A Mind-bending Road Trip to the Australian Outback.

Thanks to my most fearless critics and greatest supporters: Sarah, Holly, and Minta. Oh, and Rawcus, my muse without whom the Firefly Electrics Series would not exist.